## "How long since his dad passed?

"Two years. Grayson was seven, Bryce four," Tessa replied.

So Grayson was nine. The irony had Dirk straightening. His daughter, Emory, would've been nine if she were still here.

"I've had him in counseling for most of that time," Tessa continued, "but the older he gets, the angrier he seems."

"Because his dad is gone, and he doesn't understand why." He knew just how Grayson felt. Dirk still couldn't comprehend why his family had been taken. And he was still here.

Wrapping her arms around her middle, she nodded. "I'm hoping that spending the summer here will impact him somehow."

Dirk thought about his own ongoing recovery. Not the physical, but the mental. It had begun in earnest when he'd started woodworking again.

Was it possible something like that could help Grayson?

The sudden prodding in the area of his heart urged him to run the idea past Tessa.

"I don't know what your plans are for this summer—" he rubbed the back of his neck "—but I might have an idea."

*Publishers Weekly* bestselling author **Mindy Obenhaus** lives on a ranch in Texas with her husband, two sassy pups, and countless cattle and deer. She's passionate about touching readers with biblical truths in an entertaining, and sometimes adventurous, manner. When she's not writing, you'll usually find her in the kitchen, spending time with family or roaming the ranch. She'd love to connect with you via her website, mindyobenhaus.com.

## Books by Mindy Obenhaus

### Love Inspired

#### K-9 Companions

*An Unexpected Companion*

#### Hope Crossing

*The Cowgirl's Redemption*
*A Christmas Bargain*
*Loving the Rancher's Children*
*Her Christmas Healing*
*Hidden Secrets Between Them*
*Rediscovering Christmas*

#### Bliss, Texas

*A Father's Promise*
*A Brother's Promise*
*A Future to Fight For*
*Their Yuletide Healing*

Visit the Author Profile page at LoveInspired.com for more titles.

# AN UNEXPECTED COMPANION

## MINDY OBENHAUS

**LOVE INSPIRED**
INSPIRATIONAL ROMANCE

**LOVE INSPIRED**®
INSPIRATIONAL ROMANCE

ISBN-13: 978-1-335-93714-8

Recycling programs
for this product may
not exist in your area.

An Unexpected Companion

Love Inspired
22 Adelaide St. West, 41st Floor
Toronto, Ontario M5H 4E3, Canada
www.LoveInspired.com

Printed in U.S.A.

But the God of all grace, who hath called us
unto his eternal glory by Christ Jesus, after that
ye have suffered a while, make you perfect,
stablish, strengthen, settle you.
—*1 Peter* 5:10

For Your Glory, Lord

# Chapter One

"**D**o we have to spend the *whole* summer at the ranch?"

Her son's query had Tessa Wagner tightening her grip on the steering wheel as she propelled her Ford Explorer down the two-lane road the Tuesday after Memorial Day. Though Legacy Ranch was little more than an hour northwest of their home outside of Houston, her son Grayson's constant grousing had made today's trip seem much longer.

With a fortifying breath, she turned on her blinker before addressing the nine-year-old. "But you always look forward to spending summers at the ranch." It was one of the things she appreciated most about being a schoolteacher. The opportunity to escape everyday life and recharge. Though this year they needed this respite more than ever.

Since his father's passing two years ago, her once-happy Grayson had become a brooding shell of his former self, and no amount of counseling seemed to help. Last fall, he began acting out at school. Picking fights and walking around with what seemed like the world's biggest chip on his shoulder. If she couldn't find a way to reach him soon, Tessa feared she might lose him forever.

"But I won't get to play with my friends," he whined as she approached the ranch entrance.

Strange, she hadn't heard him mention missing his friends

before. Only since spending this past weekend with his paternal grandparents.

"I'll play with you, Grayson." Leave it to Bryce, her perpetually positive six-year-old, to try and lift his brother's spirits. "We can ride horses, go fishing and—*whoa...*"

Maneuvering her vehicle over the cattle guard beneath the arched metal sign that welcomed them to Legacy Ranch, Tessa glimpsed Bryce's wide-eyed expression in the rearview mirror. Then she spotted the longhorns grazing in the lush green pasture. In shades of black, brown, dun and white, some plain, others brindled or with spots, the cattle synonymous with Texas were always an impressive sight. One that was normally restricted to pastures along the back of the ranch while the Charolais were usually up here. Granted, Aunt Dee rotated her cattle, but Tessa had never seen the longhorns up here before.

Another look in her rearview mirror revealed Grayson's face pressed to the glass as he took in the spectacle. And if she wasn't mistaken, he wore a hint of a smile.

That made her smile. Because, at this point, she'd take what she could get.

Continuing along the winding gravel drive, she rolled down the windows, welcoming the late-May warmth into the air-conditioned vehicle while propelling the SUV up a gentle rise. Within moments, the fragrance of fresh-cut hay, earth and sunshine had the knots in her shoulder muscles loosening.

Seemed the older she got, the more she appreciated the ranch. Not that thirty-five was old, but after all she'd been through since her husband, Nick, suffered a traumatic brain injury while serving in Afghanistan—one that ultimately led to him taking his own life—she sometimes felt as though she'd lived a thousand lifetimes.

But at Legacy Ranch, her burden didn't seem so heavy. Though that could be because of her aunt. D'Lynn Hunt never let life get her down. She simply rolled with the punches. Whether it was sacrificing her life as a rancher to move to the big city and raise four girls who'd lost their mother or caring for her aging parents as their time on earth grew short, Aunt Dee clung to her faith and kept her chin up.

Bumping over another cattle guard, Tessa continued up the tree-lined path that led to the home where her father, grandfather and great-grandmother had all been raised.

"We're almost there, guys." Anticipation pulsed through her veins. *God, please let this summer make a difference in Grayson's life. In all our lives.*

When the two-story colonial-style farmhouse came into view, Tessa was met with another surprise. One that had her jaw dropping as she rounded the circle drive to stop in front of the old brick walkway that led to the porch steps.

"Aunt Dee, what have you done?"

Grayson poked his head through the front seats. "What happened?"

The century-plus-old home's tired white siding had been painted a beautiful pale gray and the black shutters given a fresh coat, along with the front door. And if she wasn't mistaken, those were new windows. The white porch rail and balusters that spanned the length of the old wooden veranda were also new additions. Traditional in style, they breathed new life into the oft-used—and now even more inviting—space.

The sound of tires traversing gravel had her turning her attention to the drive that led to the ranch's original log cabin and the east pasture. A half second later, her aunt's two-decades-old blue extended cab Chevy Silverado came into view.

Smiling, Tessa unbuckled her seat belt and opened the

door to emerge into the late-morning sunshine as her aunt brought the truck to a stop beside the six-seater utility vehicle parked beneath the ancient oak at the far end of the house.

Moments later, Aunt Dee hopped out, then waited for Nash, her tricolored blue merle Australian shepherd, to follow.

"Y'all're here earlier than I expected." Wearing dusty boots, well-worn jeans and a chambray shirt over a bright pink tank, the sixty-two-year-old woman tossed the door closed and started toward Tessa as Grayson and Bryce emerged from the back seat.

"What can I say?" Tessa shrugged as her aunt approached. "I couldn't wait to get here."

She'd wanted to come three days ago, but her in-laws had wanted one last weekend with the boys, so she'd used the time to clean her house and catch up on laundry. After a relaxing summer at the ranch, she did not want to go home to a bunch of chores.

With her shoulder-length blond hair pulled back into a low ponytail, her aunt tipped her well-worn straw cowboy hat up a notch until her faded blue eyes met Tessa's. "And I'm so glad you are." Her smile wide, she wrapped Tessa in a warm embrace. "I always miss my girls."

Releasing her, Dee turned her attention to Grayson and Bryce, who were showering Nash with affection. "I've missed my boys, too. Come here, fellas." Dropping to one knee, she opened her arms, nearly toppling when the boys eagerly complied.

While Dee was Tessa's father's sister, she was more like a mother to Tessa and her sisters, Meredith, Audrey and Kendall. They were all still in school when their mom passed away and Dee came to live with them. Then she spent the next decade raising them as if they were her own while their father continued to climb the ranks at one of Houston's largest commercial real estate firms.

Only fourteen when her mother died, Tessa had always appreciated her aunt's sacrifice. Raising four girls ranging from age eight to sixteen was no easy task. Yet Dee had never complained.

The screech of a power tool pierced the air.

"What was that?" Rubbing Nash's head, Tessa watched as Dee released the boys and stood.

"Oh, I'm just having a little work done at the log cabin."

Tessa nodded toward the house. "Like you did here?"

An uncharacteristic shade of pink crept into Dee's cheeks as she lifted her hands in surrender. "Now, I know you girls are part owners of this ranch, but this is somethin' I've been itchin' to do for a long time. But whenever I'd mention anything to your daddy, he'd always shut me down." She shook her head. "He never appreciated this place like I do, so when you and the boys went home after spring break, I got a wild hair and decided to take matters in my own hands." Palms in the air, she added, "Now, I paid for everything myself, but if you and your sisters don't like it, well, then, I guess we'll just have to figure somethin' out."

"I don't know what there is to figure out, Dee. It's gorgeous. Are those new windows?" Tessa pointed.

"Yes. Those old single-pane ones might have character, but they were so drafty it cost a fortune to heat and cool this place."

Tessa eyed the mirror-image red-brick chimneys on either side of the house. "I'm glad you didn't paint the brick."

Her aunt narrowed her gaze. "If it ain't broke, there's no reason to fix it."

Tessa couldn't help laughing as her aunt started toward the house.

"Y'all come on in, and we'll rustle up some lunch." Dee continued up the steps. "I've got some chocolate chip cookies I made before checkin' cattle this mornin', too."

"Cookies!" Both boys raced after her.

While Nash followed the trio into the house, Tessa took a moment to admire the refreshed porch up close before continuing through the front door and into the center hall of the house. The home had undergone many changes since it was built at the turn of the 20th century yet managed to retain much of its old-world charm. Like the ancient long-leaf pine floors, wood-plank ceilings and ornate fireplace surrounds.

Then she glimpsed the living room to her left, its dark wood paneling eliciting a groan. After turning the screened-in porch off of the kitchen into a family room in the early 1970s, Tessa's grandfather had finished it out with paneling. Then, apparently, liked it so much, he repeated it in the living and dining rooms, leaving them dark and dated. Not to mention, rarely used.

With a sigh, she continued through the hall, passing the straight staircase. Not much had changed since her grandparents died within months of each other six years ago. But with Aunt Dee overseeing the three-thousand-acre ranch all by herself, she didn't have a lot of extra time to devote to the house. The land was her passion, and she gave it everything she had.

Inside the familiar kitchen with chipped lemon yellow countertops, Nash sat at the boys' feet, seemingly hanging on their every word. Tessa had always loved this space. It was the original farmhouse kitchen with a mix of stained and painted wood cabinets, open shelving, a vintage butcher-block island and old crocks brimming with timeworn utensils, like her grandmother's favorite wooden rolling pin.

While Aunt Dee pulled bread, lunch meat, cheese and

condiments from the white top-mount refrigerator, Tessa retrieved plates from the cupboard to the left of the original farmhouse sink as the boys climbed into two of the four wooden captain's chairs positioned around the matching table. Thankfully, Grayson's grousing had subsided. For the moment, anyway. Perhaps now that they were here, he'd be so preoccupied that he'd forget about whatever he imagined he might be missing at home.

After lunch, they enjoyed some of Dee's cookies before the boys went their separate ways. Bryce played with his great-grandfather's Tinkertoys on the floor in the adjacent family room, while Grayson and Nash went exploring outside, granting Tessa some time alone with her aunt.

"How're things with Grayson?" Dee fingered the crumbs on her napkin.

Tessa could only shrug. "Ever the contrarian. He's not happy we're staying here for the entire summer."

Dee's brow pleated. "But he loves comin' out here."

"I know. To hear him, though, you'd think it was torture."

She patted Tessa's hand. "Give him a few days. He'll get over it."

"I hope so." Tessa slouched as tears stung the backs of her eyes. "I just don't know how to reach him anymore. He's always angry. And he's not even close to being a teenager."

"His daddy's death did a real number on him." Dee watched her. "On all of you."

The front door slammed, propelling both women from their chairs. Tessa swiped the moisture from her cheeks as she followed her aunt into the hall, where they found a red-faced Grayson, back pressed against the solid door as his chest rose and fell with each rapid breath.

"What's going on?" Tessa approached, giving him a visual once-over. "Are you hurt? Where's Nash?"

Just then, a scratch sounded from the other side of the door.

Dee opened it and waved the dog inside. Then paused, peering through the opening. "Dirk?"

"Afternoon, Ms. D'Lynn." The male voice was followed by the sound of boots ascending the porch steps.

And while Tessa didn't recognize the voice, Grayson's eyes widened. He was ready to bolt, but Tessa caught him by the arm as Bryce came up behind them.

"I didn't do anything." Grayson attempted to pull away.

Tessa maintained her grip. "Then where are you going?" And what had he done?

When Dee swung the door wide, a man with sandy blond hair and a short, scruffy beard stood on the porch, a black-and-white border collie at his side. And it was wearing a service vest.

Her aunt glanced from him to Grayson and back. "Is there a problem?"

"I'm not sure. Molly—" he gestured to the dog "—and I spotted this young man at the cabin." He nodded in Grayson's direction, his biceps straining the sleeves of the gray T-shirt that topped his dusty jeans. "When I asked if he needed help, he claimed his mom owned Legacy Ranch and then ran away." He turned his attention to Aunt Dee. "Since I haven't seen him before and—to my knowledge—you don't have any children, I thought I'd best check things out with you."

"I appreciate you lookin' out for me, Dirk. I should've let you know I had company comin'." The way Dee's gaze darted between Tessa and Grayson had Tessa's cheeks heating. Especially when her aunt waved the man and his dog inside. "Dirk Matthews—" she closed the door "—this is my niece Tessa, and her sons, Grayson and Bryce. They're visitin' for the summer." She turned her attention to Tessa and the boys. "Dirk is doin' some work at the cabin."

"I see." Feeling a smidge of relief, Tessa managed a smile. "It's nice to meet you."

He nodded. "Likewise." Drawing in a breath, he turned his gray-blue eyes back to Dee. "Thank you for clearing things up. Now that I know who's who, I'll get back to work." He reached for the door, then paused, his gaze moving to Grayson. "Say, I, uh, seem to have misplaced my laser measure. I left it on the tailgate of my truck. I don't suppose you saw a small black and red box-like device, did you?"

Grayson lowered his dark brown eyes, shifting from one sneaker-covered foot to the other. "No."

Mr. Matthews nodded. "I guess I'll just have to keep looking, then."

As he tugged the door open, Tessa noticed a bulge in the side pocket of Grayson's basketball shorts. Strange, she hadn't noticed it before. And his phone—the one she only allowed him to carry when they were apart—was still in her purse. Sure, he could've picked up a rock or some other fascinating piece of nature while he was outside, but her gut told her otherwise. And while she hated doubting her son…

"What's in your pocket, Grayson?"

His wide-eyed gaze jerked to hers. "Nothing."

"If that's the case, then show me what it is, please."

*"Mom—"*

*"Now*, Grayson."

With one hand still on the doorknob, Dirk watched as the boy struggled to comply with his mother's edict. Though Dirk already knew the outcome.

He and Molly had been eating lunch inside the one-room log cabin when Nash strolled in, looking for a handout. That was when Dirk spotted Grayson near his truck. And he had no idea where the auburn-haired boy had come from.

So he'd stayed just inside the cabin, watching the boy explore the items Dirk had on his tailgate. Until Nash barked, drawing attention to Dirk and startling the boy, who then dropped whatever had been in his hands. After hastily picking it up, he'd shoved it into his pocket before announcing that his mom owned the ranch and Dirk couldn't do anything to him. Then he bolted.

While Nash had followed the boy, Dirk could only wonder if Grayson did, in fact, belong on Ms. D'Lynn's property. And when a quick inspection of his truck revealed Dirk's laser measure had disappeared, he knew something was amiss.

Now he watched as the boy tugged the device from his pocket, his cheeks ruddy, a frown on his face. "I just wanted to play with it."

"It's a tool, not a toy." Wearing denim shorts and a modest purple tank top, his mother took it from him, her annoyance evident in her flared nostrils. "One that doesn't belong to you." She handed it to Dirk, swiping her light brown waves behind one ear. "Please make sure it's still in working order. If not, I'll pay for a replacement." Glaring at her son, she added, "And then make Grayson work it off."

While Dirk appreciated the gesture… "I'll have to do a calibration test and get back to you."

The younger boy—Bryce, was it?—stepped closer and peered up at Dirk with curious brown eyes. "Can I pet your dog?"

Dirk felt a tug at the corners of his mouth. Even on his worst day—and he'd had his fair share of those since the accident—he couldn't deny the kid. "Thank you for asking first. Yes, you may. Her name is Molly." He'd gotten the service dog while being fitted for his prosthetic. Not only did she help Dirk with his balance and retrieving, she gave him something to focus on beside himself. And brought him back to reality whenever memories of the night he lost his wife and daughter—along with the lower portion of his left leg—threatened to pull him under.

"She's soft," the boy said as Ms. D'Lynn's dog nudged him with his nose.

"Looks like Nash is jealous," she offered.

"That's okay." Bryce set his free hand atop the dog with different colored eyes. "I can pet both of them."

"You've got a couple of happy pups there, Bryce," said Ms. D'Lynn.

Dirk eyed Grayson, who remained beside his mother, watching Bryce enjoy the dogs. Making Dirk wonder if it was anger that still had Grayson sulking or a squelched desire to join his brother.

"Can I go to our room?" Grayson frowned at his mother.

"You may." Tessa lifted her chin. "After you apologize to Mr. Matthews."

The kid's body seemed to deflate as he took a sudden interest in the blue, beige and brown Oriental rug beneath their feet. "Sorry I took your thing."

Dirk hated to think ill of the kid, but he'd been young once. He knew the only thing Grayson was sorry about was that he'd gotten caught. Still, Dirk wasn't mad at the boy. "Perhaps we'll meet again, under better circumstances."

Grayson turned then, rounded the banister and started up the stairs.

"While you're up there," his mother called after him, "you can unpack your suitcase and put your clothes away."

His mission complete, Dirk turned his attention to Ms. D'Lynn. "I'd best be getting back to work." With a nod toward Tessa and Bryce, he added, "It was nice to meet all of you." He reached for the door. "Come on, Molly. We've got work to do."

Outside, they continued down the steps, Dirk absently rubbing a thumb over the device he still held. He'd give it a once-over later.

He strode past Ms. D'Lynn's utility vehicle and truck, then along the leafed-out crepe myrtles at the corners of the well-worn path that led to the cabin he'd started on only late last week. The motherly rancher had hired him to transform the old log structure—the ranch's original home turned hunting cabin—into an inviting getaway for guests. That meant redesigning the crude bathroom layout, as well as adding a small but usable kitchen, a means of heating and cooling and stairs to the loft. But if he could transform a dilapidated barn into a home for himself, he could do just about anything. Which was why he'd given up architecture to focus on building and restorations.

Gravel crunched beneath his work boots while cattle lowed in the pastures beyond the barbed wire fencing that flanked his path. Try as he might, though, he couldn't stop thinking about Grayson. What would make a kid who couldn't be more than ten behave with such disrespect? As though he was mad at the world.

Sadly, Dirk was all too familiar with that kind of anger. To this day he couldn't understand why he was still here while his wife, Lindsey, and daughter, Emory, were gone forever. Every time he put on his prosthetic, he was reminded of that horrific night. The driving rain. The semi. The terror that had enveloped him as their vehicle tumbled down that embankment.

If it hadn't been for Molly, his parents and his faith, Dirk would still be carrying that anger around with him every day. A heavy load for even the toughest adult. But Grayson was just a kid. Did he feel neglected? Was he crying out for attention? Yet his brother seemed to be a typical carefree child?

Dirk shook his head. He didn't have much insight into kids. His daughter had been only four when she died. And though his brother, Jared, had a six- and eight-year-old, Dirk wasn't around them all that often.

The afternoon sun grew more intense by the minute, so Dirk was grateful when he saw the front yard of the log cabin bathed in shade from the live oak that was likely as old as or older than the cabin itself. He had to admit, Ms. D'Lynn's family had done a good job of caring for the structure that had been built sometime in the 1800s. The chinking had been maintained, and he'd found very little rotted wood.

When a wet nose touched his hand, he looked down at Molly and smiled at the pup who was good at anticipating his needs. "I'm alright, girl." He rubbed her head. "But you're probably ready for some water, aren't you?"

He continued onto the porch, where he retrieved his two-gallon water jug. And after adding a measure of the cool liquid to Molly's bowl, he chugged some himself. Until he heard the humming of an engine.

Lowering the container, he saw a six-seater utility vehicle approach. And Tessa was behind the wheel.

She parked and turned off the motor before starting his way holding something in her hands. Her light brown waves grazed her shoulders and swayed back and forth with each step while her hazel eyes were fixed on him. Making him wonder if he'd done something to upset her.

So he remained where he was with a panting Molly.

"I brought you some cookies." Tessa smiled easing his angst. "Aunt Dee—D'Lynn—made them this morning." Continuing onto the porch, she handed him the foil-covered paper plate. She was a petite thing. At five-ten, he towered over her.

"Thank you." He set his jug aside before peeling back the foil and grabbing one of the chocolate chip treats. "Care to join me?"

"No, thank you. I've already had more than enough." Crossing her arms, she rocked back on the heels of her slip-on sneakers. "Any verdict on your laser thing?"

He grinned, setting the plate aside, making sure it was out of Molly's reach. "Laser measure. And no, not yet." He took a bite of the cookie, the burst of chocolate satiating his sweet tooth.

Tessa nodded, studying the cabin's facade. "This place used to intimidate me. But it's kind of like being transported to another place in time."

"Not when I'm finished with it." He took another bite.

"What?" Her curious gaze jerked to his.

Shaking his head, he swallowed. "Don't worry, all of its charm will remain, just more suited to modern tastes. Basically, your aunt wants to make it a usable space."

"I can appreciate that." Nodding, she glanced from the old home to the live oak, appearing somewhat hesitant. As if there was something she wanted to say but was holding back.

And when Molly inched closer to press against Tessa's leg, he was convinced.

"I get the feeling you didn't come down here just to bring me cookies." To emphasize his point, he shoved the rest of the treat in his mouth before dusting the crumbs from his hands.

"No, I did not." One hand falling to Molly, Tessa took a deep breath, then let it go with a huff. "While I'm not one to make excuses for my children's actions, I feel compelled to tell you that Grayson hasn't always been the brooding bundle of antagonism you witnessed earlier. He's…changed since his father's death. And to be honest, I'm not sure how to help him."

Dirk almost choked on the cookie. He swallowed hard. "How long since his dad passed?"

"Two years. Grayson was seven, Bryce four."

So Grayson was nine. The irony had Dirk straightening. His daughter, Emory, would've been nine if she was still here.

"I've had him in counseling for most of that time." Tessa continued petting Molly, and as she stared into the trees, Dirk wondered if she was even aware she was doing it. "But the older he gets, the angrier he seems."

"Because his dad is gone, and he doesn't understand why." The words tumbled out before he realized he'd said them aloud. But he knew just how Grayson felt. Though Dirk was much older, he still couldn't comprehend why his family had been taken and he was still here.

Wrapping her arms around her middle, Tessa nodded. "I'm hoping spending the summer here will impact him somehow. That I'll find some way to reach him."

Dirk thought about his own ongoing recovery. Not the physical, but the mental. It had begun in earnest when he'd started woodworking again. His mother had wanted a rustic dining table, so he'd built one for her. It wasn't long after that he decided to turn an old barn on their property into a home for himself, and thus began his career as a woodworker and contractor.

Was it possible something like that could help Grayson? Make him feel as though he had purpose?

The sudden prodding in the area of his heart urged him to run the idea past Tessa.

"I don't know what your plans are for this summer—" he rubbed the back of his neck "—but I might have an idea."

One brow lifted. "I'm listening."

He lowered his hand and looked her in the eye. "What if

Grayson helped me here? I mean, this cabin is a part of his legacy, too. Knowing that he's doing something meaningful might give him a new perspective."

The corners of her mouth twitched before flattening once again. "*If* he embraces the idea. Otherwise he'll only end up being more trouble for you."

"He probably won't be enthused at first. But if we can make him feel like he's a part of something or that he's making a difference, that may be all it takes to get him going. Plus, it'll be something only he gets to do. Not him and Bryce."

A breeze whispered through the leaves as she worried her bottom lip. "You know, you may have hit the nail on the head with that last part. The boys are almost always together." She met his gaze. "I'll agree to this arrangement on one condition."

"Which is?"

"If Grayson doesn't listen to you, defies you or argues with you, that you will let me know. Because I don't want you or your work to suffer."

"I can do that."

She continued to watch him, the lines on her brow relaxing. "In that case, when do you want him to start?"

"How about tomorrow? That'll give me time to find some suitable projects for him."

Wrinkling her nose, she said, "I hope I didn't coerce you into this with my whining."

"I don't think you were whining at all. You're a mom desperate to help her son. And in the process, presented me with an opportunity to serve."

"I guess we'll find out tomorrow."

## Chapter Two

Had she lost her mind?

Tessa climbed the front porch steps at her aunt's a little after two, wondering what was wrong with her. She'd just agreed to let her son work alongside a perfect stranger. For all she knew, Dirk Matthews could be a serial killer. The quiet, unassuming type who lived a nomadic life, roaming the country, looking for his next victim.

He was the one who'd suggested Grayson work with him, after all. Just because Dirk looked innocent—perhaps even compassionate—didn't mean it wasn't an act. She'd glimpsed something in the depths of his gray-blue eyes that suggested all wasn't right with Mr. Matthews. At first, she'd shrugged it off, but the more she thought about it, the more it unnerved her.

No, before she'd let Grayson help Dirk at the cabin, she needed to learn more about him. And who better to ask than her aunt.

"You're back," Dee said when Tessa walked into the kitchen. "Dirk said you were on your way."

She'd talked to Dirk? "Why didn't you just call me?"

"I did. You left your phone here." She pointed toward the table on her way to the laundry room that opened onto the old carriage porch along the back half of the house. Shoving her sock feet into her boots, her aunt continued. "Anyway, Gentry called. I got a heifer that's havin' a hard time calving, so I need to get out there." She straightened. "The boys are both upstairs. They're bein' quiet, probably starin' at some electronic device. Though they oughta be outside. But with Grayson in trouble, well…" She shrugged. "I thought we'd grill up some burgers for supper. Meat's in the fridge. Canned beans and some chips in the pantry, though you're welcome to whip up whatever you like. I invited Dirk and Gentry to join us, so if I'm not back, go ahead and start fixin' things without me. Hope I won't be that long, but you never know with heifers."

Reeling from Dee's monologue, Tessa grabbed hold of the counter. "You invited Dirk?"

"I did. After what happened today, he deserves a little show of appreciation."

Which was why Tessa had taken him the cookies. But that was before he suggested Grayson help him at the cabin. "How well do you know Dirk?"

"I met him when he came out to bid on the job at the cabin. Gentry recommended him. He and Dirk's daddy grew up together over in Whisper."

Tessa didn't care what had gone on in the tiny community several miles down the road. She cared about the safety of her children. So even though Gentry was Dee's right-hand man here at the ranch, one her aunt trusted implicitly and whose opinion she valued, Tessa's consternation remained.

"The poor fella looks down in the dumps half the time." Dee snagged her hat from the hook by the door and set it atop her head. "But I reckon he's got good cause."

"Why's that?"

Dee's smile disappeared. "According to Gentry, Dirk lost his wife and little girl in a car wreck several years back."

Tessa felt her eyes widen. "His wife *and* child?"

"Part of a leg, too."

Was that why he had a service dog? He didn't look like he needed any assistance. Then she recalled the way Molly had encouraged Tessa to pet her. As if sensing her turmoil.

Dee sighed. "I can't imagine the kinda pain that man has endured." Her gaze drifted to Tessa's. "Though I reckon you might have some inklin'."

Nick's death had certainly wreaked havoc with her emotions. But she'd had to keep going for her boys. To give them the best life she could. Without them, she'd have been a worthless heap.

"To a point, I suppose."

Dee's phone buzzed. She tugged it from her back pocket to look at the screen. "It's Gentry. Impatient man. I need to go."

Nodding, Tessa said, "That's alright. We'll be fine."

When Nash started to follow, her aunt held out a hand. "Stay, boy. That heifer's stressed enough without you runnin' around." Halfway out the door, she poked her head back inside. "By the way, this spring's haul of dewberries is in the freezer if you're inclined to make cobbler for dessert." Grinning, she waggled her eyebrows.

"Do you have any Blue Bell?"

"Homemade Vanilla."

"Good. Now go help Gentry and don't worry about supper. I'll take care of it."

Dee closed the door, and Tessa watched her go, her mind racing. In a matter of moments, she'd gone from convincing herself Dirk was a serial killer to empathizing with him. Losing Nick had dealt her a massive blow. But right now, it paled in light of what Dirk had been through. The loss of a limb would've meant physical pain in addition to the agony of losing his family.

And yet he'd offered to help Grayson.

Her gratitude returned in full force. Now she had to tell Grayson he'd be working with the man. She didn't want to do it while Bryce was around, though. He'd only ask to join them. And Dirk was right, Grayson needed some time away from his brother. An opportunity to feel like he was a part of something.

"Come on, Nash. Let's go check on the boys." The old dog moseyed up the stairs ahead of her, to the largest of the four bedrooms on that level. The one with pale blue walls that not only overlooked the backyard but boasted a set of bunkbeds in addition to the queen-size bed.

Sure enough, both boys were on their bunks, staring at their tablets. She should've thought to take Grayson's as part of his punishment.

"How come you guys aren't outside exploring?"

"'Cause I'm in trouble." Grayson's eyes never left his device.

"Then why are you playing with this?" Reaching over the rail of the top bunk, she took the tablet from him.

"Hey." He sat up with a scowl.

Her gaze fell to the bottom bunk. "Bryce, what are you doing up here?"

"Keeping Grayson company."

She shook her head. "Have you both unpacked?"

"Yes," came the collective reply.

"Yes, ma'am, please."

"Yes, ma'am."

"That's better. Now come downstairs. Aunt Dee had to go help Gentry with a heifer that's having trouble calving—"

"Ohh, can I see?" Bryce bounded to his feet, his pleading hazel eyes staring up at her.

"No. Even Nash had to stay behind. The heifer might be

in distress, so they can't risk agitating her." That could mean losing the calf. "But with Aunt Dee gone, we're in charge of dinner."

"You mean supper," said Bryce. "Aunt Dee always calls dinner supper."

Tessa ruffled his light brown hair. "You are correct."

"What do *we* have to do?" Grayson all but groaned as he descended his bunk.

"I'm sure Nash would like to play ball. And we need to make sure the grill is clean."

"Can we eat outside?" Bryce about bounced out of his sneakers. "We always do that here."

"Alright. But we'll need to make sure everything is clean. The table, chairs."

"We can do that, can't we, Grayson?" Bryce peered up at his brother, mischief glinting in his eyes. "Maybe we can use the hose."

Grayson demonstrated the enthusiasm of a slug. "Whatever."

"You'd better put your swim trunks on, then." Either one or both of them was bound to end up soaking wet. "And Grayson?"

He looked up at her. Something he wouldn't be doing much longer at the rate he was growing.

"Stop feeling sorry for yourself. You were the one who made a poor choice. So don't take it out on the rest of us."

Thirty minutes later, armed with a bucket of soapy water and the hose, the boys set to work on the patio while Tessa watched them from the kitchen as she made cobbler and potato salad. Yet with all of today's events churning through her mind, it was Dirk who kept rising to the surface. And for the first time, she recognized that look in his eyes. The one that had unnerved her. It was the same one she'd seen every time she looked in the mirror in the months following Nick's death. That look of pain, confusion and uncertainty swirling together, making you wonder if anything would ever be normal again.

The boys' laughter echoed from outside, making her smile. They all needed more laughter in their lives. Grayson, in particular.

By six fifteen, everything but the meat was ready. Now Tessa was debating whether to go ahead and cook the burgers or wait for Dee. Her phone beeped then, and she pulled it from her pocket to see a text from her aunt.

Mama and calf are doing fine. Headed your way.

"That answers that question." Dilemma solved, she joined her freshly clothed boys outside where they were playing cornhole in the shade-covered St. Augustine grass alongside the patio area. Grayson's mood seemed much improved. And for that, she was thankful.

"When are we gonna eat?" Her ever-hungry eldest looked her way.

"Soon. Aunt Dee just texted that she's on her way back." She paused beside the wood-pellet grill. "But there are some carrots and hummus on the counter, if you need a snack."

"'Kay." Grayson started toward the house.

"Wait for me." Bryce tossed his beanbag aside and chased after his brother.

After making sure the hopper was full, Tessa ignited the grill.

"I thought I heard voices back here."

She turned at Dirk's comment while Nash trotted toward Molly, his tail wagging.

Dirk's hair was damp and combed back. He'd also traded

his work clothes for a heather blue T-shirt and khaki shorts that revealed his prosthetic leg. Yet for as much as she didn't want to, she found herself staring.

*Shake it off, Tessa! He's a normal guy.*

One she'd imagined to be a serial killer a few hours ago. Was that messed up or what?

She cleared her throat. "I'm just firing up the grill." Her lame attempt at casual had her sounding like a flustered schoolgirl. "My aunt texted. She's on her way."

"I guess I am a little early." He glanced at his watch. "She said six thirty. How'd things turn out with that heifer?"

"Good. Mama and baby are fine."

He shifted his sneaker-clad feet, bearing his weight on his good leg. "Glad to hear it."

Hoping to sound like the intelligent woman she was, she said, "Any verdict on your laser thing?"

Lips pressed together, he nodded. "Let's just say the prognosis isn't good. I think the sensor may have been damaged."

She cringed. "I'm sorry."

"Hey, you two."

They turned at Dee's voice.

She stopped beside their guest. "Glad you could make it, Dirk."

"I appreciate the invitation."

With a glance Tessa's way, her aunt said, "If y'all don't mind, I need to grab a shower. The only thing worse than sweaty is sweaty and gritty, and that's what I am."

The boys' chatter had the adults looking toward the house as Grayson and Bryce pushed through the back door.

"Hey, fellas." Their aunt started their way, taking in the patio as she went. "Y'all did a good job of cleanin' things up out here. Looks great."

Grayson's smile had disappeared as he descended the steps. His gaze repeatedly darted to Dirk.

"I'd give you a hug," her aunt continued, "but that'll have to wait until after my shower." With a glance over her shoulder, she said, "Y'all go greet our guest. Gentry'll be along in a bit, too."

While Dee went into the house and Bryce joined Tessa and Dirk, Grayson hung back.

"What happened to your leg?" Bryce peered up at Dirk.

"I was in a car accident." Dirk didn't elaborate.

"Oh." Bryce looked from Dirk's shoes to his face. "Does it hurt?"

"Not anymore. And my prosthetic—" he gestured to the artificial limb that extended from his knee "—allows me to walk just like anyone else."

"That's good." While Bryce had no problem approaching Dirk, Grayson had yet to join them, and Tessa couldn't help wondering if he was ashamed of his earlier actions or, perhaps, intimidated by Dirk's prosthetic. Or Dirk, in general.

Before she could encourage him to join them, Dirk approached Grayson.

"Look, Grayson, I know we didn't get off to the best start this afternoon, so perhaps we could try again." He held out his hand. "I'm Mr. Dirk. And I'm looking forward to working with you at the cabin."

Tessa's heart skidded to a momentary halt. Grayson didn't know he was going to be working with Dirk because she hadn't told him yet.

"Working?" Confusion contorted Gray's face.

"Yeah," said Dirk. "Helping me update the cabin."

Tessa joined them, watching her son's gaze dart between her and Dirk, as if they'd been plotting a conspiracy. "Um, I haven't had an opportunity to tell Grayson yet." Turning her attention to the boy, she said, "I told you that you would have to work toward the cost of replacing the tool you took from Mr. Dirk. He suggested you could help him at the cabin."

The tips of Grayson's ears turned red, along with his cheeks. "That's not fair. It's summer vacation. I should get to do whatever I want." He crossed his arms over his chest, his gaze darting to Dirk's prosthetic. "I'm not gonna work for him."

Tessa mimicked his stance. "Yes, you are. You took something that didn't belong to you and then you broke it."

"Tessa, it's okay." Dirk stepped between her and her son. "You can find another way for him to work it off. I'm not going to force him to help me."

With a huff, Grayson turned and stormed toward the house, the wooden screen door banging behind him as he stepped inside.

Beside her, Dirk scrubbed a hand over his face. "I'm sorry. I assumed he knew."

"It's not your fault. You were only trying to help." Just like she was. Yet Grayson seemed to be drifting further and further away. And she didn't know what to do. She only knew that she did not want to lose her son the way she'd lost Nick.

Dirk arrived at Legacy Ranch early the next morning. With so many distractions yesterday, he hadn't accomplished near as much as he'd hoped. That, coupled with last night's disaster at Ms. D'Lynn's, had made it difficult to sleep.

To say supper had been a fiasco would be an understatement. All because Dirk had opened his big mouth in an effort to smooth things over with Grayson. If Gentry hadn't shown up shortly after the boy stormed off, Dirk might not have stayed.

Grayson had never returned, whether by choice or his

mother's insistence, Dirk couldn't be sure. All he knew was that he was to blame.

So when Ms. D'Lynn called while he was picking up lumber from the building supply this morning, informing him that Grayson would be joining him at the cabin after all, Dirk was more than a little surprised. And wondered whose idea it had been, Tessa's or her aunt's. Because Dirk was certain it hadn't been Grayson's.

Now, as the sun rose higher, Dirk unloaded the last of the two-by-fours from his truck, Molly flanking his left side, in case he lost his footing. Something that didn't happen as often as it had early on in their relationship.

Between mourning the loss of his wife and daughter and suffering more than one infection in his stump, he'd spent a lot of time lying around, wishing God would've taken him, too. Until he met Molly.

His physical therapist was Molly's trainer. And from their first meeting, Molly refused to leave him alone. She'd set her head in his lap or nudge him with her nose as if to say *Come on, you can do this.*

Despite being a medium-sized dog, Molly hadn't let that deter her from assisting him. She seemed to will herself to stand taller and held her head high. Whatever gap needed to be filled for him to lead a normal life, she was determined to do it. And her persistence had encouraged him to press on.

As he added the boards to the existing stack alongside the covered porch, he hated to think where he'd be without her.

When he straightened, the sound of a vehicle approaching had his muscles tightening.

Soon, Ms. D'Lynn's Silverado came into sight.

*Lord, please, don't let me blow it again.*

She eased to a stop alongside Dirk's truck and turned off the engine.

He watched as she glanced past Nash, who sat beside her, to the boy in the passenger seat, curious as to what she might be saying. She didn't strike him as harsh or prone to belittling. Though she wasn't one to hide her expectations, either. If she could make ornery cowboys do her bidding, a nine-year-old boy didn't stand a chance.

Finally, they emerged from the vehicle.

"Stay," Dirk commanded Molly as Nash bounded their way.

"Mornin', Dirk." Clad in faded Wranglers, boots and a well-worn chambray shirt, Ms. D'Lynn paused near the hood of her truck and waved as she waited on her nephew.

"Morning, Ms. D'Lynn." Dirk patted his hip as he descended the two steps, signaling Molly to remain close. They continued across the dew-covered grass, his gaze moving to the boy clad in jeans and a red T-shirt. "Grayson, how are you doing today?"

The kid gave him a tentative look. "Okay, I guess."

Dirk squinted against the sun peering through the leaves. "I'm glad you could join me. Are you ready to build something?"

The boy shoved his hands in his pockets and looked from Dirk to his aunt. "I don't know how to build stuff."

Dirk moved closer, out of the sun, noticing the way Molly kept looking from him to the boy, no doubt sensing Grayson's unease. "That's alright. I'll teach you."

"Oh, I almost forgot." Ms. D'Lynn scurried back to her truck and reached into the bed. A second later, she returned, holding a small cooler. "Grayson, your lunch is in here, along with plenty of water. Make sure you stay hydrated."

"Yes, ma'am."

So the kid did have manners. Quite a change from the

defiant boy Dirk had witnessed yesterday. But then, Ms. D'Lynn could be intimidating.

She handed Grayson the cooler before starting back to her truck. "I'll check on y'all later." Reaching for the door, she glanced their way. "Come on, Nash."

Grayson watched his aunt drive away, looking as uncomfortable as a wool suit in August. So Dirk signaled Molly to go to him.

While she nudged the boy's hand, Dirk turned and started toward the cabin. "Why don't you find a shady spot for that cooler, and we'll get to work."

The kid lugged it to the porch, Molly between them. "What are we gonna do?" He set the container down.

"We're going to start framing the walls for the kitchen and bathroom." Dirk paused at the door to the cabin. "Come on, I'll show you."

Inside the one-room log structure with a loft, a stone fireplace and a makeshift bathroom, he continued to the worktable he'd set up on the far side of the fireplace and retrieved his tablet. A few taps later, he pulled up the 3D rendering of his design. "This'll show you what things are going to look like when the job's finished."

The boy's eyes widened with something akin to interest. "How'd you do that?"

"Computer program. I used to be an architect, and this is how I designed homes."

"Are those stairs?" The boy pointed to the screen.

"They sure are." Dirk eyed the old wooden ladder leaning against the loft. "I'll be building those this week, too. Perhaps you can help me."

Grayson reached for Molly. "I don't know how."

"Like I said, I'll teach you. That is, if you'd like to learn."

When the boy didn't respond, he added, "But if you don't want to, that's okay, too."

The boy looked around the space, then back at the screen. "I guess it would be okay."

"In that case, let's get to work."

Grayson helped him move the two sawhorses from the porch to the grass, then Dirk retrieved his circular saw from the back of his truck, along with a tape measure. Next, they worked as a team to move a small stack of two-by-fours to the sawhorses before returning to the cabin.

"Before we can cut we have to measure how long our boards need to be." In a structure like this, they could all be different.

He took the tape from his belt and measured the height first, Grayson watching him. "This is where I would typically use my laser measure."

The boy's shoulders slumped. "Is that the thing I broke?"

Dirk regretted his choice of words. "Yes."

Grayson's gaze fell. "I'm sorry." His tone reflected a sincerity that hadn't been there yesterday.

"I know you are, Grayson. And I trust you're going to make better choices going forward."

Petting Molly, he sent Dirk a curious look. "How come you're not mad at me?"

"I was never mad at you. I just couldn't understand why you did it."

"Because I'm *stupid*." The kid kicked at a board.

Dirk gave the boy his full attention. "An error in judgment does not make you stupid." He'd certainly done some things he wished he could take back. Such as arguing with Lindsey while driving sixty miles an hour on the interstate in a rainstorm.

Grayson lowered to one knee, wrapping his arms around Molly's neck. "My dad said I was."

The words were barely audible. If they hadn't been inside the house, Dirk would have missed them. And while a part of him wished he hadn't heard them, they'd given him some valuable insight into this, seemingly, tormented little boy.

Was Tessa aware her late husband had said such a thing?

Dirk stooped so he was eye-to-eye with the boy. "Grayson, I may not know you very well, but you are *not* stupid. You got that?"

The boy watched him for a long moment before nodding.

"Good. Now that we've got that settled, let's get to work." As Dirk straightened, he was all too aware that working on this cabin had suddenly become more than just a job. It had become a mission.

# Chapter Three

Tessa couldn't recall the last time she'd been alone, especially here at the ranch. Yet with Dee out and about doing who knows what, Grayson at the cabin with Dirk, and Bryce riding shotgun with Gentry as he searched for that heifer and her calf to make sure they were doing alright, alone was exactly what Tessa was. Yet instead of savoring the all-too-rare occasion, she was fretting.

What had Aunt Dee said to Grayson that had him up early this morning, dressed and ready to help Dirk at the cabin? And then, when Tessa offered to take him, Dee had insisted Tessa stay put, that she'd take him herself.

Then again, Dee had a way of getting people to do her bidding. Only part of the reason Legacy Ranch ran so smoothly. When D'Lynn Hunt told you to do something, you did it.

Except she wasn't the one working with Grayson. Dirk was. And Tessa could only pray her son would cooperate.

Refreshing her coffee, she stared out the window over the sink to the horses grazing in the pasture beyond the backyard. She loved this view. Loved the ranch, in general. Life moved at a different pace out here. Something she was reminded of every time they visited. Which, inevitably, had her entertaining notions of pulling up stakes and moving out here for good. But how would a move like that impact the boys? While they enjoyed their visits, life at the ranch was very different than in the city. Which, she supposed, was part of the allure. Still, it would mean a new school, new friends, new church, new activities. And with the way Grayson had been behaving lately...

She sipped the steaming liquid as the sound of tires on gravel announced someone's arrival. Taking a step back, she glanced into the laundry room as Dee's truck eased to a stop alongside the carriage porch.

Moments later, her aunt followed Nash inside.

After setting her hat on a hook, Dee toed off her boots, glancing Tessa's way. "Have you heard anything from Dirk or Grayson?"

Tessa's gut tightened. "No. Why, have you?" She petted the Australian shepherd staring up at her with those multi-colored eyes.

"No, praise the Lord." Dee continued into the kitchen, heading straight for the coffeepot. "Guess that means we're alone."

A rarity, for sure. Yet as Tessa sipped her now lukewarm brew, she couldn't help wondering what had her aunt so fired up.

"Let's have a little chat." After filling her mug, Dee leaned against the counter, wearing a giddy grin.

Tessa eyed her suspiciously, wondering if she was about to be lectured on parenting an unruly child. "Anything in particular you want to talk about?"

Dee nodded. "The ranch."

While Tessa was relieved Grayson would not be the topic of their conversation, that didn't stop the knot that formed in her gut.

Setting her cup on the ancient butcher block in the middle of the space, she said, "Please tell me you're not thinking about selling." Something her father had wanted to do for ages, but Dee always refused. Had she changed her mind? Was that why she'd been having so much work done? The house, the cabin. Had the ranch become too much for her?

Of course, Tessa and her sisters now owned their father's half of Legacy Ranch—something Tessa considered much more valuable than the tidy monetary inheritance he'd left each of his daughters, as well as his sister. Which meant Dee couldn't sell unless they were all in agreement. And Tessa definitely was not.

Her aunt's face contorted. "Why on earth would you even think such a thing? You know Legacy Ranch is more than a piece of real estate to me. It's my lifeblood. That said, I have been thinkin' about makin' some changes."

Tessa's gaze narrowed on her suddenly—not to mention uncharacteristically—nervous aunt. "What sort of changes?"

After taking a long draw of her coffee, Dee said, "I'd like to turn a portion of the ranch into a country getaway."

"Country getaway? For whom?"

Lifting her chin a notch, Dee said, "For folks eager to escape the city and enjoy life at a slower pace."

"Where did this come from?" Tessa perched a fist on her hip. "Is the ranch losing money? Do you need more income?"

"No." Her aunt waved off Tessa's concerns. "You know how it goes. There are good years and there are bad years. It evens out. Like the Bible says, 'All things work together for good.'" Her faded blue eyes met Tessa's. "This is somethin' I've been itchin' to do for a good while."

"Did you mention it to Dad?"

Lips pursed, Dee shook her head. "I was too afraid. You know what they say. You gotta spend money to make money. Yet whenever I suggested anything that involved puttin' money into the ranch, my big brother always shut me down."

"But he was a businessman. Surely he could've seen the value in your idea."

"Psh." Dee moved to the table and pulled out a chair. "Your daddy had no use for this place, you know that."

Another reason Tessa was thankful Dee had helped raise her and her sisters. Unlike their father, Dee shared her passion for the land with them and saw to it they got to spend large chunks of time out here, grounding them in their heritage.

"So, tell me what you have in mind." Retrieving her cup, Tessa continued toward the coffeepot for a refill while Dee sat.

"Well, now, that's where I have a bit of a problem." She looked up as Tessa joined her at the table. "I've got too many ideas rollin' 'round this bleach-blond head of mine. Makes it difficult to nail 'em down. The only thing I was certain about was that, with a little TLC, that cabin could be a real draw."

Watching her aunt, Tessa perched her chin on her hand. "You have yet to tell me what all you're having done to it."

"Addin' a decent bathroom and a succinct kitchen." Dee lifted her cup, then paused. "And stairs to the loft. Then I'll have to do some decoratin'. Make it look nice and invitin'."

"Not to mention less scary." As a little girl, Tessa had been terrified of the crude structure. Or what she'd feared lurked inside it, anyway.

Her aunt cackled. "Your run-in with that 'coon when you were eight liked to have scared you half to death."

"It bared its teeth."

"That's cuz she had babies in there." Dee continued to laugh.

"I could've gotten rabies."

"Only if she bit you. And the way you hightailed it out of there, she didn't stand a chance."

Tessa huffed. "Okay, enough about my childhood phobias. What other ideas do you have?"

"Well, there's the old bunkhouse that I'm thinkin' might be nice for families, if it was fixed up. I've also contemplated doin' somethin' with that barn over by the buzzard's roost, but I don't know what yet." Dee lifted a brow. "And have you ever heard of glampin'?"

"I have. But the bigger question is what are people going to do while they're here?"

"Well..." Dee looked perplexed. "What do you and the boys enjoy doin' when you're here?"

Tessa shrugged. "Stuff we don't get to do in the city. Fishing. Spending the day at the swimming hole. Riding horses." She eyed her aunt. "The horse thing would probably require a *lot* of liability insurance, though. The boys like exploring. Picking stuff from your garden." She leaned back in her chair. "I'm partial to campfires. Staring up at the night sky and seeing all those stars. Sitting on the porch, doing nothing but watching the cattle or deer. Savoring the sounds of nature instead of traffic."

"Now you're gettin' somewhere, sister." Dee leaned forward with a smile. "Those last things you mentioned. The stars, nature. Sometimes it's life's simplest pleasures that bring us the most joy. Help us unwind. And if I can provide a way for folks to experience that, well, maybe I can make a difference in this world."

Did the woman have any idea what a difference she'd made in the lives of her four nieces? "So will you be granting guests free rein of the ranch?"

Her aunt sent her an appalling look. "What, do you think I was born yesterday? This is a workin' cattle ranch. I'd limit them to certain areas. Keep 'em closer to the front of the property."

Tessa lifted a brow. "Is that why you moved the longhorns near the entrance?"

Dee smiled. "You know what they say, you only get one opportunity to make a first impression."

Tessa thought about the boys' reaction when they arrived. "The longhorns will definitely do that."

Her aunt let go a seemingly nervous sigh. "So what do you think?"

"I think you deserve to have *your* dreams come true for a change. You've devoted your life to taking care of others. Me and my sisters, Papaw and Memaw. This ranch." She sucked in a breath. "But I can't speak for Meredith, Audrey and Kendall. Perhaps we could talk them into coming out here one weekend so we can discuss things with them."

Looking uncharacteristically nervous, her aunt said, "Does this mean you like my idea or you're tryin' to placate an old woman?"

Tessa couldn't help laughing. "You are far from old, Aunt Dee. You've got more energy than women half your age." Her gaze drifted to her aunt's. "It needs some fleshing out, but yes, I think it's a great idea." One Tessa could totally get on board with.

"Oh, goody." Dee all but beamed. "I'll give the girls a call tonight and see when they're available."

"You're looking at a lot of work before you can host anyone, though. Especially if you plan to do something with the bunkhouse or barn. Who would you hire to do the work?"

"If Dirk is interested, I'd stick with him. According to Gentry, he turned a run-down barn on his folks' property into a home for himself."

"Could he handle something like that?"

"I don't know. I'd have to talk with him."

Dee's phone chimed. She tugged it from the back pocket

of her jeans. "It's Dirk." Still staring at the device, she tapped the screen and said, "Hi, Dirk," obviously putting him on speaker.

There was a sigh before Dirk said, "We have a situation down here at the cabin."

Tessa's body tensed, her gaze colliding with Dee's as her aunt said, "What kind of situation?"

Another sigh. "It might be best if you just come down here. Like right now. And you should probably bring Tessa."

Her stomach churning, Tessa pushed to her feet. What had Grayson done now?

The sun filtered through the two windows on the wall behind Dirk, illuminating dust motes and making the stifling air in the cabin's loft grow even warmer. "How're you doin', buddy?" Dirk knelt on the wooden floor behind Grayson, his arms hooked under the boy's, wishing he hadn't allowed him up here. Or that he'd at least done a thorough inspection before doing so. Dirk was just thankful the boy hadn't fallen completely through to the floor below.

"Okay, I guess." Grayson's response was accompanied by a wince. And it was no wonder, with one of his legs stuck in a broken floorboard while the other contorted atop the loft floor. Dirk prayed nothing was broken.

"You deserve some ice cream after this. What's your favorite flavor?" Sweat trailing down his cheek, he mentally chided himself for the nonsensical question. But if it distracted Grayson...

"Cookies and Cream," the boy responded.

Dirk made a mental note, once again eyeing the aged wooden rafters above them. One slightly darkened spot, in particular. "Your mother and your aunt should be here any minute."

The boy groaned. "Mom's gonna be mad at me again."

"No, she won't. This was an accident." One that might have been avoided if Dirk had inspected things better. *Lord, please don't let Grayson be badly hurt.*

Molly whined somewhere below them.

Dirk could envision her staring up the ladder or pacing, bothered that she couldn't get to them. "Sorry, girl. Hopefully we'll be down soon."

*"Dirk?"* Tessa's high-pitched voice echoed from below.

"Up here." He wasn't about to let go of Grayson.

"What on earth," he heard Ms. D'Lynn say right before Tessa neared the top of the ladder. Not the rickety wooden one that had been here for ages, but Dirk's aluminum step-ladder.

"Watch where you step," Dirk cautioned her as she crawled onto the loft floor.

Her hazel eyes widened when she spotted her son. "What happened?" She continued toward them on all fours.

"I wanted to see the loft." There was a hint of a whimper in Grayson's tone.

"I'm sorry, Tessa." Dirk met her gaze as her aunt appeared behind her. "I've been up here before and thought it was sound. While sitting here, though, I noticed a spot on the ceiling that's darker than the rest." He nodded toward the ceiling. "Water must've leaked in and rotted the floorboard."

"Can you pull him out?" The worried look on her face as she knelt beside him cut him to the core.

"When I tried, he yelped. Said something poked him in the leg. Might be a splinter." He prayed it wasn't a nail. "I need someone to check down below to see if it can be cleared before I try again."

"I'll go do that." Ms. D'Lynn returned to the ladder.

Assuming a cross-legged position beside Dirk, Tessa

smoothed a hand over her son's hair. "Hang in there, Gray. We'll figure this out just as quick as we can."

She smelled of coffee and something sweet.

As if he had any business noticing.

"Grayson?" Ms. D'Lynn hollered below them a few moments later.

"Yeah?"

"I'm gonna start feelin' around your leg. You let me know if somethin' hurts."

"'Kay." Within seconds, the boy snickered. "That tickle— ow!"

"I found the problem," the boy's aunt hollered. "There's a chunk of wood wedged—I just need to—"

Grayson hissed.

"Got it!" she hollered. "See if you can get him out now."

"Alright, Grayson, let's try this again." Dirk eyed Tessa. "If you wouldn't mind spotting me."

As she stood, Dirk tightened his hold and lifted the boy until his foot had cleared the hole.

Tessa grabbed her son and pulled him aside while Dirk crawled away from the weakened spot.

Pushing to his feet, Dirk said, "How's he doing?"

Back on her knees, she examined Grayson. "He doesn't seem to have any trouble standing on it." She met her son's gaze. "Are you hurting anywhere?"

"Just a little right here." Grayson rubbed his thigh.

"Let me take a look." She ran a finger over the spot. "There's a small tear in your jeans."

"Might be where that chunk of wood poked him." Ms. D'Lynn watched them from the ladder.

Dirk moved beside Tessa and her son. "If it broke the skin, you might need to get him checked out. I'd hate for him to get an infection." No telling what could be lurking in rotted wood in a house this old. "There's an urgent care center up the road in Hope Crossing." He'd pay for it, of course.

"Grayson, you'll need to pull your pants down so I can see."

*"Mom!"* A horrified Grayson looked Dirk's way.

Hoping to hide his grin, Dirk started toward the ladder. "Holler when you're ready to come down so I can spot you."

Ms. D'Lynn was waiting when he reached the bottom, Molly at her side. "I don't understand. I've walked that loft multiple times in recent months and never noticed any problems up there. Matter of fact, Gentry and I hauled out the old bed just a few weeks ago."

After assuring Molly he was alright, Dirk continued toward the underside of Grayson's mishap to check out the damage. "I should have caught it when I inspected things prior to starting the job." Just the way he should've noticed that semi veering into his lane. Shaking off the memory, he peered up at the jagged hole just big enough for a little boy's foot.

"How could you when there were no obvious signs?" Ms. D'Lynn countered.

"We're coming down." Tessa's voice had Dirk returning to the ladder, where Grayson had begun his descent. When her gaze met Dirk's, she added, "The skin was not broken."

*Thank You, God.*

"What's goin' on? Y'all havin' a party without us?" Gentry strolled in the front door with a curious Bryce at his side. The old cowboy nudged his dirty straw Resistol back farther, revealing his salt-and-pepper hair. And when he spotted Ms. D'Lynn, his smile grew a little wider.

Dirk would ponder that observation another time.

"You gentlemen missed all the excitement." Ms. D'Lynn hugged her youngest nephew.

With Grayson safely on the cabin's lower level, Molly leaned into him while Dirk waited for Tessa as Bryce scurried their way.

"I wanna go in the loft."

"No!" Dirk and Tessa insisted simultaneously.

Ruffling her youngest's hair, she said, "It's not safe up there right now."

"What happened?" Gentry's smile evaporated as Ms. D'Lynn filled him in.

"You're kiddin'." Removing his hat, Gentry scratched his head. "I didn't see any problems last time I was up there."

"Me, neither," said Tessa's aunt. "But we're gonna need to get that roof repaired toot sweet."

"You know, you could swap out that shake roof for a metal one," said Gentry.

Casting a disgusted look Gentry's way, Ms. D'Lynn perched a fist on her hip. "And sacrifice the character of this cabin? I don't think so."

The old cowboy frowned. "Alright. I reckon me and Dirk can handle it."

Gentry assumed Dirk would still be around. But after what just happened, he might be out of a job.

With both the front and back doors open, a breeze sifted through the cabin as Gentry, Ms. D'Lynn and the boys went outside. Meanwhile Tessa held back.

Dirk wouldn't blame her for being upset with him. He was pretty annoyed with himself. Working alone was one thing, but when he had someone else with him—especially a child—he needed to be more vigilant.

Rubbing Molly's head, he cleared his throat. "Tessa, I'm sorry for putting Grayson in danger."

Her light brown waves swayed as she shook her head. "You didn't know the floor had been compromised."

"No, I didn't. But I should have." He dragged a hand through his hair, narrowing the distance between them. "Perhaps it would be best if Grayson didn't help me anymore. I'd hate for him to get hurt."

"I'm not hurt." Grayson strode through the door and toward them, his bottom lip protruding. "You just don't want me here anymore 'cause I caused trouble."

"Trouble?" Dirk stared at the boy as Molly moved between them. "Not at all. You were eager to learn and more than happy to help. I'm the one who invited trouble by not making sure the loft was secure."

Crossing her arms, Tessa watched Dirk. "And just how would you have done that?"

"I'm—"

"Were you up there with him?" She cocked her head.

"Yes, but—"

"And did you see anything unusual?"

"No, but then—"

Her brow furrowed. "Stop beating yourself up, Dirk. Accidents happen."

He knew that all too well. An accident had cost him his family.

"What's all the hollerin' about?" Ms. D'Lynn stepped inside the front door.

Tessa looked at her aunt. "Would you please tell Dirk that what happened was not his fault?"

The older woman turned a perplexed gaze his way. "Your fault? I own this cabin. And I've spent a lotta time in it recently, pacin' the floors, decidin' what I wanted done. And there wasn't a thing that woulda had me suspectin' there was a problem with that floor. What happened today was an act of God, you got that, Dirk?"

It was no wonder Ms. D'Lynn had no problem getting her hired hands to do her bidding.

With Molly again at his side, he said, "Yes, ma'am."

"Good, 'cause I'm countin' on you to make my vision for this place a reality. Matter of fact, I might be needin' your help on another project once you finish this one. That is, if you're interested."

Dirk knew Ms. D'Lynn was a feisty one, he just hadn't realized how feisty. He wasn't sure he'd ever been so properly put in his place before. And it humbled him.

His gaze drifted to a pouting Grayson. Earlier, Dirk had thought of working with Grayson, helping him overcome his anger, as a mission. If that's what it was, then why was he ready to give up so quickly?

*Because you're making it all about you.*

*God, thank You for protecting Grayson.* The boy really had been an asset during the short time they'd spent together today. He was surprisingly conscientious and took instruction well. Just what Dirk had been hoping for when he'd made the suggestion to Tessa yesterday.

Clearing his throat, he turned his attention back to Ms. D'Lynn. "Yes, ma'am, I believe I would. But if you all will excuse us, Grayson and I need to get back to work."

# Chapter Four

While Aunt Dee was out and about the ranch and the boys continued to sleep, Tessa roamed the living and dining rooms shortly after eight Saturday morning, mug in hand. Despite the bright morning sun, the rooms felt dreary thanks to the paneling that was every bit as dark as the coffee in her cup and covered every single wall, sucking the life out of what should be two inviting spaces.

Based on her research, she had two options. Remove the paneling or paint over it. But before a decision could be made, she needed to know what was beneath it. Hopefully, her aunt would know. Once that was determined, the next step would be convincing the cowgirl to let Tessa do the work. It would be a labor of love, for sure. But she had two months to knock it out. And she was certain the results would be worth any amount of effort.

Continuing to pace the worn dusty-rose carpet that should also be banned, she thought about her favorite home improvement shows. How they'd take a depressing old home and turn it into something spectacular. That was precisely what she wanted to do here. Now that Dee had spruced up the outside, why not do the same inside.

Movement beyond the window had her glancing that way as Dee's truck eased up the drive.

Moments later Tessa greeted her and Nash in the kitchen. "You're back awfully soon."

"Forgot my thermos. This old body needs more caffeine. I'm not used to stayin' up so late." Her aunt whisked past her to palm the stainless steel cylinder on the counter. "Boys still asleep?"

"Yes, ma'am." It had been almost midnight by the time they got to bed. Dee had made a fire in the pit in the backyard, so they'd toasted marshmallows, hunted for fireflies and worn themselves out in the process.

"I also needed to drop off Nash. I'm cuttin' hay in the north end pasture today. So, if you need me, just gimme a call."

Moving to the coffee pot for a refill, Tessa eyed her aunt over her shoulder. "Hey, before you head out, I have a proposal for you."

"Well, that would be a first."

Tessa returned the carafe to the burner, chuckling at the comment. Dee was a confirmed bachelorette. Said she never found a man worth the effort.

"Follow me." Tessa crossed the kitchen and continued through the door to the dining room with her aunt and Nash on her heels, then veered left into the adjoining living room.

"May I, please, either paint or remove the paneling in these two rooms? It would brighten this house up considerably and bring these spaces into the twenty-first century."

Her aunt's brow furrowed. "You sure you wanna spend your summer doin' that?"

"I can't think of anything I'd rather do."

"Well…" Her aunt scrutinized the two rooms. "It sure would perk up these depressing spaces." Returning her attention to Tessa, she added, "We might even want to use them again."

Tessa thought she might burst with excitement. "There's just one thing I need to know."

"What's that?"

"Do you have any idea what's behind the paneling? That's going to determine if I paint over it or remove it."

Contemplating the question, Dee twisted the lid off of her thermos and took a swig. "It's been this way for so long, but near as I can recall, it was just Sheetrock before. Like's in the center hall and my bedroom." Her bedroom sat on the opposite side of the hall from the living room in what had once been the parlor. Until Memaw wanted a downstairs bedroom and Papaw turned the space into a main suite.

"In that case, I'll plan to remove the paneling." Catching herself, Tessa worried her bottom lip. "That is, if I have your approval."

"Sweetpea, you're welcome to do whatever you like. This house is long overdue for a makeover."

Tessa clapped her hands. "Yay!" She hugged her aunt. "Thank you."

"What are you thankin' me for? You're the one who'll be doin' all the work. Unless you can get your sisters to help."

Aunt Dee had FaceTimed Meredith, Audrey and Kendall Wednesday night and they'd agreed to come to the ranch next weekend.

"Good idea."

"And your boys, too."

Tessa shook her head. "No. No painting for them."

Just then, Grayson and Bryce's voices echoed from the stairs.

"Oh, good." Dee started toward the entry hall. "I can get me some hugs before I head back out."

When her aunt left, Tessa set to work on the French toast and bacon the boys requested. Seemed last night had left them with hearty appetites. Her, too. When she finally joined them at the table, Grayson was explaining to his brother what he and Dirk had done these past few days. She couldn't help smiling when he used words like "studs" and "framed out." As if he was some master builder.

Working with Dirk had been good for him. She'd never considered how the lack of male influence might be impacting Grayson's life. And the work helped keep him busy, too.

"When are we going to the rodeo?" Bryce used his fork to drag a bite of French toast through the layer of syrup on his plate.

"Not until later this afternoon."

"Can I do the mutton bustin' again?"

"That's for babies." Beside her, Grayson smirked as he took a bite of his bacon.

And just when she thought his attitude was improving.

"Nuh-uh." Bryce scowled at his brother across the table. "You're just jealous cuz you can't do it anymore."

Her youngest had likely pegged things correctly. Grayson used to beg to get on the back of a sheep and hold on for dear life. And still prominently displayed the blue ribbon he'd won his final go-round three years ago. Nick had been there to watch his son compete and celebrate with him. She'd never imagined that would be the last time they'd attend as a family. Nick never joined them at the ranch again. Instead, he'd become withdrawn and had started drinking regularly.

Shaking off the unwanted memories, she said, "That's enough, you two." She looked from Grayson to his brother. "To answer your question, Bryce, yes, I will allow you to participate."

"Will Aunt Dee watch me?"

"Oh, yes. I'm sure you'll hear her cheering you on from the bleachers just the way she has every other year." Tessa wasn't sure what she'd do without her aunt. The woman was her rock.

Once they'd finished eating, she said, "You boys go get dressed while I clean up the kitchen. Then you can take Nash outside and check the garden to see if anything needs picking."

Alone, she set to work loading the dishwasher, willing thoughts of those last tumultuous months with Nick to that dark corner in the back of her mind. Then she chose to focus on the living and dining rooms. She could hardly wait to get started. The first thing she'd have to do was remove that paneling. She supposed she'd have to study it for a while, determine how it had been attached and go from there.

She was closing the dishwasher when the doorbell rang. Retrieving the dish towel from the counter, she wiped her hands. And by the time she moved into the center hall, the boys were racing down the stairs.

"Who is it?" Bryce asked.

"I don't know yet." Since it was a solid door without sidelights, she had no way of knowing who was on the other side. Perhaps she should talk to Dee about a new door. One that not only allowed you to see who was there but granted some much-needed light to the dim space.

Grayson leaped from the bottom step and jogged into the living room to peer out the window there. "It's Mr. Dirk."

That seemed to bring a smile to his face.

She unlocked the door before opening it wide. "Good morning."

"Morning." His gaze fell to the boys, who were beside her now. "Grayson. Bryce." He nodded, Molly at his side. And she wasn't wearing her vest.

"Come on in." She held the door wide.

Both boys gave Molly a rub, which had Nash drawing near, looking for some attention of his own.

"What brings you by?" She closed the door and peered up at him. "You're not working at the cabin today, are you?"

"No. However, I was going through my toolbox and came across this." He held up the emergency phone she'd given Grayson, his attention shifting to her son. "I thought you might need it."

"Thanks." Petting Molly with one hand, Grayson took hold of the device with the other, glancing her way with a rather sheepish expression. Yes, they would be having a discussion about responsibility later. "I forgot I put it there."

"At least it was in a safe place." The look Dirk sent her seemed to implore her to give the kid a break.

"Mr. Dirk, I'm gonna do mutton bustin' at the rodeo tonight." Pride sparkled in Bryce's brown eyes as he peered up at Dirk.

"You are? I used to do that when I was about your age."

"You did?"

Dirk nodded. "I even won a time or two."

"Me, too." Grayson puffed out his chest.

"Are you going to the rodeo?" Bryce asked Dirk. "Cuz you can watch me."

Dirk rubbed his beard. "As a matter of fact, I was thinking about heading out there tonight. But now that I know you're going to be competing, I'll be there for sure."

Tessa felt her heart trip. Would he really go because her son had asked him?

When his gray-blue eyes drifted to hers, she averted her gaze to the living room. And one glance at that dark paneling had her thoughts shifting gears.

"Boys, if it's alright with Mr. Dirk, why don't you take

the dogs out back with you while you check the garden. I
need to talk to Mr. Dirk for a minute."

Grayson shifted his attention to Dirk. "Can we?"

"Sure. Molly's off duty at the moment, so she'd probably
enjoy running around with you kids."

"Cool." Grayson took off down the hall. "Come on Molly.
Come on Nash."

The dogs' paws tapped out a rhythm on the wood floor
as they followed, while Bryce chased after them.

As they headed out the back door, Dirk looked her way.
"Did I say something wrong?"

"No. Not at all. Matter of fact, it would mean a lot to Bryce
if you were there to watch him." She sucked in a breath. "But
I do have something I'd like to talk to you about." With that,
she started into the living room, motioning for him to join
her. "I despise this paneling. Aunt Dee says there's Sheetrock behind it. What I'm curious about is how difficult it's
going to be to remove the paneling."

Moving closer to the wall, he smoothed a hand over the
veneer as he studied it. "It's been nailed on." He glanced over
his shoulder at her. "It's possible they also used glue." He
stepped back, taking in both rooms before addressing her.
"When was this house built?"

"Around 1900."

"Do you know if there's anything behind the Sheetrock?"

She shook her head. "I could ask Dee. Why?"

Still studying things, he said, "A house like this, from that
era, could have shiplap."

"Shiplap? Seriously?" Again, her mind went back to those
home improvement shows and the owners' delight when
they'd find the vintage wood boards buried beneath a wall.
Talk about a treasure.

"Wouldn't surprise me in the least."

She couldn't help grinning. "That would be amazing. How do we find out?"

After a thoughtful moment, he said, "I could remove a light switch or electrical plate and have a look behind them."

Tessa couldn't recall the last time she'd been this giddy. "Yes, please. I mean, if you have time."

He chuckled. "Sure. Let me go get my toolbox."


"Way to go, Bryce! Now smile and hold up that blue ribbon while I take your picture." Surrounded by a pleasant early June evening and the earthy smells of livestock and dust, Dirk watched as Tessa aimed her phone at her youngest, her proud smile the biggest he'd ever seen. And rightfully so. From the moment the handlers set her son atop that sheep, Bryce had clung to the ewe for all he was worth. Now he was the mutton bustin' champion of this year's Hope Crossing Fair and Rodeo.

"I am so proud of you, kiddo." Ms. D'Lynn moved from her spot between Dirk and Gentry to give her great-nephew a hug while his mother studied the photos she'd taken. "Was it fun?"

"It was awesome!"

"You were pretty awesome yourself." Gripping the rigid handle extending from Molly's vest, Dirk held up his other hand for a high five, and the boy promptly obliged.

"I can't believe I'm the mom of *two* mutton bustin' champs." Tessa beamed. "Grayson, get in there with your brother so I can get some shots of you two together." Seemingly satisfied, Tessa tucked her phone inside her purse minutes later. "So what would you boys like to do? Stay and watch the rodeo or go do something else?"

"I wanna ride the rides." Grayson's uncharacteristic en-

thusiasm—at least in the brief time Dirk had known him—
had him bouncing on the balls of his cowboy boots.

"Me, too." Bryce nodded. "And I want cotton candy."

"I'm hungry for some kettle corn." Ms. D'Lynn wore
a flowing black short-sleeved shirt over stylish jeans and
turquoise-colored Ariats, while turquoise earrings dangled
from her lobes beneath a straw hat adorned with a matching beaded band.

Beside her, Gentry couldn't seem to stop staring. "Sounds
good to me." If the look on his face was any indication,
the woman could've requested worms and the old cowboy
would've agreed.

The boys raced ahead as the group turned away from
the outdoor rodeo arena to make their way across the fair-
grounds toward the carnival area, the sun slowly descending behind them. The adults, on the other hand, moved at a
more leisurely pace, Molly aiding Dirk as he maneuvered
the uneven terrain.

Glancing at a smiling Tessa, he was reminded of this
morning at Ms. D'Lynn's house. He'd never seen someone
so excited over shiplap. On TV, perhaps, but not in person.
Yet when he'd given her the news that, buried beneath lay-
ers of paneling and Sheetrock, her aunt's home did, indeed,
possess the overlapping wood planks, Tessa had been downright giddy. And he couldn't recall the last time he'd heard
such a sweet sound.

Her giggles had touched something long dormant inside of
him. Something he shouldn't be dwelling on. Yet he'd found
himself doing just that all day.

Meanwhile, he had yet to tell her what Grayson had said
that first day he'd joined him at the cabin. About his father
telling him he was stupid. Dirk still couldn't understand why
anyone would do such a thing. Words often left kids with

deep, lingering wounds. And based on some of Dirk's observations this week, he suspected that might have something to do with Grayson's anger issues.

Now, as the sounds of the carnival grew louder, Bryce said, "I want to ride the Ferris wheel." He eyed his brother. "Wanna ride with me?"

Though Grayson tried to act nonchalant, there was a spark in his eyes that suggested he was just as eager as his little brother.

"What about me?" Wearing a sleeveless, belted denim dress with cowgirl boots, Tessa looked almost disappointed. "You don't want me to ride with you?"

Without the slightest bit of remorse, her youngest shook his head. "I wanna ride with Grayson. But you can ride with Mr. Dirk."

Alone in a small gondola with Tessa? Dirk wasn't sure how he felt about that. "What about Molly? She can't go on the Ferris wheel."

"I'll keep her." Leave it to Ms. D'Lynn to rob him of his excuse. Though he was sure she was only trying to be helpful.

Glancing Tessa's way, he shrugged. "I'm game if you are."

Screwing up her face, she eyed her sons. "I'm not sure how I feel about these two riding alone."

"Aw, come on, Mom," said Grayson.

"Please." Hands clasped, Bryce pleaded.

Continuing to watch them, she said, "You promise to behave? You need to sit still, and no making the gondola swing."

"But that's the best part," said Grayson.

She glared at her eldest.

With a sigh, he said, "O-kay."

While Dee and Gentry went in search of kettle corn with

Molly, Dirk started toward the Ferris wheel with Tessa and her sons. Other than the couple in front of them, they were the only ones in line. Though people began filing in behind them as the first couple stepped into their gondola. And by the time two teenagers exited the next one and Tessa's boys hopped in, the number of people waiting had grown considerably. So much so that after Dirk and Tessa were belted in, the worker stopped each and every gondola, allowing people to exit and enter. Leaving Dirk and Tessa in awkward silence while party music blasted from nearby speakers, filling the gap between them.

"That's great that Bryce won," Dirk finally said.

"Yeah. Now his brother can't lord his win over him anymore." She shook her head, the sweet aroma of her shampoo enveloping him. "There can be a fine line between competitiveness and being mean-spirited." Looking at him now, she added, "And it's one Grayson often straddles."

Deciding that may be his best segue, Dirk cleared his throat and sent up a silent prayer. "Grayson said something the other day that's been weighing heavy on my heart." Looking at the boy's mother, he continued. "I don't want to break any confidences, so I'd appreciate it if you wouldn't mention this to him, but I think it might offer some insight into his anger."

Her concerned hazel eyes bore into him as she seemed to steel herself. "Okay. I promise to keep it between us."

Taking a deep breath, he leaned closer. "He'd made a comment about being stupid. I confronted him and insisted he was not. But then I heard him mumble under his breath that his dad said he was."

As they began to move once more, Tessa lowered her head and sighed, seemingly unsurprised. When they stopped again seconds later, their gondola swayed.

"I don't normally tell people this," she started, "but my husband didn't just die. He chose to leave us."

Confusion had Dirk narrowing his gaze. "What do you mean?"

"My husband took his own life." The pain in her eyes seemed coupled with resignation. "Nick had suffered a traumatic brain injury while serving in Afghanistan. The TBI resulted in him being medically discharged from the army." She glanced at the darkening sky. "He struggled with civilian life yet refused to get the help he needed. His frustration led to him becoming angry. And while he never hurt me or the boys physically, his words were often verbal darts."

She stared in the distance as they moved and stopped again. "Eventually, Nick started drinking to numb his pain and irritation. The night he died, we argued. He walked out." Her gaze fell to her clasped hands. "Later that night, the police found him in his truck with a self-inflicted gunshot wound."

The pain in her voice had Dirk longing to hold her. Instead, he covered her hands with one of his.

She sucked in a breath and released it. "Sometimes I wonder if he wanted to transfer his pain to me. Make me hurt the way he did. But mostly I blame myself for not forcing him to get the care he needed but was too proud to accept."

"It's not your fault." He cringed at the words people had told him countless times, yet he still struggled to believe. "Sorry, I know how shallow that statement might seem. But believe it or not, I understand just how you feel."

She looked at him now, curiosity lining her brow. "How?"

As they stopped and started a couple more times, he briefly told her about the accident that had cost him so much. "Lindsey and I had been arguing right before the accident. I'll always wonder, if I hadn't been upset, would I have seen that semi veering into our lane sooner? Would my response have been different? Could I have saved my family?"

As they neared the bottom, the ride began to move in earnest.

Meeting Tessa's gaze, he said, "I've never told that last part to anyone. But I suspect you get it, don't you?"

Her gaze held his. "Yes, I do." The corners of her mouth twitched. "I'm sorry for your loss, Dirk. But I have to admit, it's oddly comforting to meet someone who can truly grasp what I went through. What I'm still going through. Thank you for sharing that, Dirk. I know it wasn't easy, but it means a lot to me."

Relief sifted through him. And as the sun dipped below the horizon, he no longer felt like a pariah. Instead, he felt less alone. Like someone else understood him. And that made him smile.

## Chapter Five

Tessa awoke the next day with an inkling of something she feared long gone. Hope.

All this time, she'd thought no one could understand what she'd gone through. The depth of guilt and pain she'd carried since Nick's death.

Dirk got it, though. Got her. And that brought a measure of comfort she hadn't possessed in a very long time. Because while her family loved her and would do anything for her, they couldn't relate the way Dirk was able to. Losing a loved one was never easy, but when tragedy was involved, it added insult to injury. Leaving one to wonder how they could've prevented something so horrific. Blaming yourself and wondering if you'll ever feel normal again.

In her heart, she knew she'd done everything she could to get Nick the help he needed. But it hadn't been enough. And she didn't want her or her boys to have to deal with those feelings of abandonment ever again.

Now, as she stood in the living room Sunday afternoon, alongside her aunt, Grayson and Bryce, that hope mingled with anticipation and had Tessa bouncing on the balls of her sneaker-clad feet. Last night—after that serendipitous Ferris wheel ride—Dirk had offered to help her start the process of removing the paneling. And she'd readily accepted.

She watched him gently tap the pry bar until it was wedged between the six-inch baseboard and paneling.

"This is boring." Grayson turned to Aunt Dee. "I thought we were gonna go get more ice cream."

Reeling him in for a hug, her aunt said, "Hold your horses, Gray. This may not seem like a big deal to you, but gettin' rid of this old paneling is monumental to your mama and me."

On his knees, Dirk looked their way. "Sorry to get your hopes up, Ms. D'Lynn, but I'm afraid the paneling won't be coming down for a while. Not until the baseboards and other trim are gone, and I'm taking extra care removing them, so they won't get damaged."

Her aunt's brow puckered. "Well, phooey. I was hoping for instant gratification."

"I'll do my best to remove at least one panel today, along with whatever's behind it so you can get a glimpse of what's beneath it all."

"In that case—" Dee turned her attention to her nephews "—boys, you want to ride to Brenham with me?"

"Yes!" They responded in unison.

Knowing her sons, they were probably hoping to talk their great-aunt into buying them more than just ice cream at the large supermarket.

While Molly's focus remained on Dirk, Nash pushed to his feet and started after them.

Dee halted and held up a hand. "Stay, boy." She rubbed his head. "I'll be back shortly."

The seemingly dejected canine sighed and plopped down on the carpet again.

Tessa turned her attention to Dirk. "How can I help?"

"I've got this first baseboard loosened. If you want to grab the other end, we'll go ahead and remove it."

She crossed to where he was working and crouched alongside one end of the board, eyeing the nails that still stretched between it and the paneling before taking hold and wiggling it free.

After marking the back of it, Dirk signaled Molly to his side before pushing to his feet and transferring the board to the other side of the room.

Watching him, Tessa said, "If you have another pry bar and hammer, I'm more than happy to help. After all, I wasn't expecting you to do any of this."

"Ah, I don't mind." He grinned behind that dark blond beard that looked as though it had been trimmed. "I'm kind of eager to see what's buried back there, too."

Stooping, he rummaged through his toolbox. "Here you go." He handed her a slightly smaller pry bar and a hammer. "You can start working on that casing." He pointed to the passage between the living room and entry hall. "The switch plates and outlet covers will need to come off, too." He again reached into the toolbox. "Here's a screwdriver for those."

"Sure thing, boss." Excitement zipped through her as she set to work.

For the next hour, the rat-a-tat-tat of hammers filled the space.

Having worked up a sweat, Tessa swiped the back of her hand across her brow. "Care for some iced tea or water?"

"Tea sounds great."

"I'll be right back, then." When she returned, she found Dirk standing in the middle of the space, staring at the paneling.

"Is something wrong?" She handed him a mason jar.

"Not at all." He took hold, his gaze skimming the wall. "I'm just evaluating. Once I remove that crown molding, we'll be able to take off one of these panels." He thumped it with a finger.

"And the Sheetrock?" She sipped her own drink.

"I'll score it with my utility knife. Prying out the first piece will be the toughest."

"We should probably wait until Dee gets back for that. Given how disappointed she was."

"That's alright." He glanced at their ongoing work. "There's still plenty to keep us busy."

After chugging half of his drink, he said, "Did y'all go to church this morning?"

"Oh, yes. Aunt Dee is adamant."

He eyed her curiously. "Don't you attend church at home?"

"We do. With all that's happened these past few years, it's even more important to me that the boys are grounded in faith."

"And what about your faith?" The intensity of his gaze was a little unnerving.

"I have faith." Aware she wasn't being completely honest, she stared into her glass. "Or used to, anyway." Trusting God had once come easily to her. Until Nick got injured. Even then, she'd clung to the belief that God had a plan.

Standing between them, Molly nosed her hand, and Tessa readily gave in to the dog's persistence as she recalled those dark days after Nick was medically discharged and they returned to Houston. While Nick never had any problem finding work, holding on to a job proved difficult. And the more frustrated and depressed he grew, the more he refused any assistance available to him.

Fighting to keep her family afloat had her faith waning as her prayers remained unanswered and Nick turned into someone she barely recognized. God could've stopped Nick from taking his own life. But He hadn't.

"Tessa?"

She looked at Dirk. "Do you ever find yourself asking God why?"

He snorted. "All the time. Not that I've ever received an answer."

She dragged her fingers through her hair and turned away. "Annoying, isn't it?"

"I suppose. I've learned something, though."

Glancing his way, she said, "What's that?"

"Questioning God's sovereignty can be exhausting. But trusting Him brings hope."

She allowed the statement to tumble through her mind. "Kind of like the whole 'Be still, and know that I am God' thing?"

He nodded. "I spent years asking 'why' and 'what if,' only to grow more frustrated. It wasn't until I let go of all those questions and began taking God at His word, believing that somehow, He still had a plan and a purpose for my life the way His word promises, that I finally found peace in my circumstances."

He moved closer. "I know your situation is different than mine. Grayson and Bryce—their futures—must weigh heavily on you. But if you will entrust them to God…"

"I—*we*—actually did that." She blinked away the unwanted moisture blurring her vision. "When they were babies, Nick and I dedicated them at our church." She still remembered standing at the altar with their pastor as he prayed over their family. She'd been so happy. So full of hope.

Since Nick's death, though, her prayer life had become a series of shotgun prayers. Brief appeals sent up, asking God to do this or that. When was the last time she'd really talked to God? Asked Him to guide her, and then trusted Him to be her sustainer and lead her so she could lead her sons?

"Somewhere along the way, I stopped trusting God and only trusted in myself." She lifted her gaze to Dirk's. "And you're right, it is exhausting."

"Jesus said, 'Come unto me, all ye that labor and are heavy laden, and I will give you rest.' Sounds like you could use some rest, Tessa."

Mere inches separated them as she stared into his gray-blue eyes. "You have no idea."

Nash barked, startling her.

Tessa glanced toward the window as Dee's truck rolled up the drive. "They're back."

"In that case, I will give you this." He handed her his mason jar and reached for the folding ladder leaning against the opening to the dining room, bringing Molly to his side. "Once I remove the crown molding, we'll attempt to eliminate one of the paneling sheets."

"We're back," Bryce announced from the kitchen. Moments later he joined them. "Aww." His shoulders fell. "The paneling's still here."

"I'm working on it." Dirk grunted from atop the ladder while Molly stared up at him.

"They're not done," Bryce announced as Dee and Grayson appeared behind him.

"Looks like they're gittin' close, though." Her smile wide, Aunt Dee clasped her hands against her chest.

"Yep," said Dirk. "We're almost there."

With the crown molding gone, Dirk moved the ladder aside and worked to pry one of the wood panels loose. "Tessa, if you'll don my work gloves—" he nodded toward the pair on the floor "—I'm going to have you hold this while I work on the other side."

"Sure thing."

Moving to the other side, he shimmied the pry bar into place and loosened things from bottom to top.

"I feel it shifting." Tessa tightened her grip.

Moments later, Dirk moved the four-by-eight panel into the entry hall while the rest of them stared at the off-white wall.

"Well. It's a start." Aunt Dee rubbed her hands together. "But I'm itchin' to see what's behind that Sheetrock."

Armed with a utility knife, Dirk made a few slices in the wall, then began prying the pieces away. "Ladies, we have shiplap." Grinning, he moved aside as Tessa approached the opening he'd created.

Her heart dropped when she glimpsed the vintage pale pink and sage green print. "That's not shiplap. It—it looks like wallpaper."

"Yes, likely with a cheesecloth-type backing." Dirk sounded as if it was no big deal. "Exposed shiplap is a recent trend. Back in the day, it was used to create a smooth backing for wallcoverings. But it's always been there, just waiting to be accessed." The upward tilt of Dirk's lips suggested he was referring to more than the shiplap.

He was right. God was still there, ever present, waiting for her to come to Him. Yet instead of taking her burdens to the One who could truly help, she'd erected a wall of self-sufficiency. One that was every bit as flimsy and ugly as that paneling she detested.

Perhaps it was time to tear down the wall she'd built around her heart and start trusting in the One who'd promised He would never leave her or forsake her.

Dirk swept the inside of the log cabin late Wednesday afternoon, while Grayson played fetch with Molly outside. After helping him all day, they both deserved a break. Besides, ever since the boy began helping Dirk, he'd observed Molly's interest in him. Dirk suspected his canine friend sensed Grayson's internal struggles. And being a trained professional, Molly wanted to help.

Setting the broom in the corner of the cabin, Dirk continued outside, closing the door behind him. "Time to call it a day."

"Already?" The boy watched as Dirk retrieved Molly's vest from atop the cooler.

"What do you mean already?" He waited as a panting Molly hurried toward him, then clipped on her vest. "It's almost five o'clock." Not that his workday was over. Just as he'd done the past two evenings, he'd go directly from the cabin to the ranch house, where Tessa would feed him supper in exchange for his continued help in the living room. Her hope was to have all of the paneling and Sheetrock in that room gone by the time her sisters arrived this weekend. And Dirk had found the task far more enjoyable than going home to an empty house. Even if it meant working in close proximity to Tessa. How the woman could sweat and still smell so good was a mystery.

Grayson approached. "Doesn't seem that long."

"Time flies when you're having fun, I guess." Dirk had enjoyed having the boy around. Surprisingly, Grayson had never complained about working here instead of enjoying his summer break. Together, they'd accomplished a good bit in the past week. The bathroom and kitchen had been framed and the electrical wiring had been run. The plumber was scheduled for tomorrow, then the drywall would go up. They'd also built and, with Gentry's assistance, installed the new staircase to the loft, and Dirk had repaired the loft floor.

Still, Dirk didn't want to eat up any more of the kid's summer than necessary. Hands on his hips, he peered down at the boy. "I have good news."

Grayson sent him a curious look.

"You've done enough work here to cover the cost of the laser measure."

The kid's smile evaporated, uncertainty swimming in his dark eyes. "Guess that means you don't want me helping you anymore." Shoulders drooping, he kicked at a tuft of grass with his sneaker.

Molly returned to the boy, nudging his hand with her nose.

"No, it means you don't *have* to help me anymore. However, if you *want* to continue working with me, that's okay, too." Dirk had already gotten Tessa's approval. "I'll even pay you."

"You don't have to pay me." A tentative smile returning, the boy gave into Molly and began stroking her fur. "I like building stuff. It's fun."

"I'm glad to hear that. But I'll still pay you."

The sound of tires on gravel had them glancing toward the road as Ms. D'Lynn's truck appeared from the pasture in a cloud of dust.

Moments later, she eased the vehicle to a stop and hopped out. "Looks like I'm just in time."

"You didn't need to come down here." Dirk grabbed his toolbox, bringing Molly to his side as he started toward his truck. "I'd have brought Grayson to the house."

"That's not why I'm here." Tanned hands perched on her denim-clad hips, she looked up at him beneath the brim of her straw hat. "I was wonderin' if you'd be willin' to take a look at somethin' for me. Give me your input."

"Sure. When?"

"Now's as good a time as any." She glanced toward the cabin. "Assumin' you're done for the day."

"We are."

"In that case, hop in your truck and follow me." She started toward her own vehicle.

"Can I come?" Grayson looked from Dirk to his aunt.

"Course you can," his aunt tossed over her shoulder.

"Can I ride with Dirk?"

Dirk met the older woman's gaze over the hood of her truck. "Fine by me."

She waved her acknowledgment as Dirk opened the door. Grayson bounded into the back seat, Molly on his heels. Then Dirk slid behind the wheel, fired up the engine and got the air conditioning flowing before following Ms. D'Lynn.

"Are those your fishing poles?"

Dirk eyed the rearview mirror to see the boy staring at the rods cradled in the overhead rack. "They are."

"You like to fish?" Grayson's eyes were wide.

"I do."

"Me, too. Maybe we could go fishing after supper."

While Dirk was grateful the boy's good mood had returned, he said, "I promised to help your mom again tonight. But we'll go one day soon."

"Tomorrow?"

Dirk couldn't help chuckling. "Let's see what your mom has to say first."

He followed Ms. D'Lynn down what appeared to be a less traveled path before spilling into another pasture. One with a large wooden gable barn that looked almost as old as the log cabin. Despite the rusted metal roof and missing time-worn boards, it was a good-looking structure. With a shimmering pond sitting just beyond, it was a picturesque setting.

Dirk stopped alongside Ms. D'Lynn's vehicle, then stepped out as Grayson and Molly bolted from the back seat. Easing toward the older woman waiting beside her front bumper, he eyed the structure fringed by spindly blackjack and post oaks and knee-high grass. "Nice barn."

"I've always thought so." Smiling, she took in the structure. "As a little girl, I used to climb up in the hayloft and hide from my brother. But after Daddy built the big metal barn closer to the house, this one was ignored." She looked at Dirk. "This one's got character, though."

"Old barns have a unique appeal." He should know, since he lived in one. And while they might not look like much from the outside, the guts of the structure—the hand-hewn posts and beams—brought an old-world charm to even the most modern spaces. "What is it you'd like me to help you with?"

"I want to know if this barn is salvageable. I mean, I know the outside is a mess, but what about the inside? Is it structurally sound?"

"Let me go take a look."

"I wanna come." Grayson started after him.

"No!" Dirk and the boy's aunt said simultaneously.

"Your mama would have my hide if I let you go in there." Ms. D'Lynn set an arm around the boy's shoulders. "You stay with me."

"Fine," he lamented.

After retrieving Molly's handle from the truck and attaching his to her vest, Dirk picked his way through the weeds until they reached the building. Inside, an old, rusted tractor sat in the center of the space while sunlight shone through the multiple gaps left by missing boards, affording him enough light to recognize that, while the outside might not be in the best shape, the structure appeared to be in good condition.

Lifting his gaze, he eyed the hayloft, as well as the trusses peppered with barn swallow nests. He pulled out his phone and zoomed the camera lens as close as he could and took a photo. Then stared at the screen, expanding it for a better look.

Just as he suspected. What was likely the original shingle roof remained and the metal roof had been laid over it, affording the interior an extra layer of protection.

"What do you think, Molly? Kind of brings back memories of our place." Though this barn was larger.

Rejoining Ms. D'Lynn and Grayson, he said, "Good news. Not only is it salvageable, the interior is in excellent condition."

The smile that bloomed on the woman's face was priceless. "Hot dog!"

"Do you have something particular in mind for this place?"

Pink blossomed on her cheeks as she waved a hand. "Just curious if it's worth hangin' on to."

The sound of an engine had them looking up the path as Tessa and Bryce came their way on the utility vehicle.

Stopping alongside them, Tessa cast them a suspicious look. "What are you all doing over here?"

"Don't worry, Grayson stayed right here by me while Dirk went inside the barn." Ms. D'Lynn knew her niece well.

Wearing shorts and a gray T-shirt with an elementary school logo, Tessa gaped at him. "You went inside that thing?"

"Sure. It's actually in very good condition."

"Mom." Grayson approached the utility vehicle. "Can Mr. Dirk and I go fishing tonight?"

Dirk cringed. Bryce was right there. He didn't want him to feel left out.

"I wanna go, too." Obviously Tessa's youngest had no problem speaking up for himself.

She glanced from one boy to the next. "I guess we have been spending a lot of time indoors lately."

"I can't leave you to tackle the living room alone," said Dirk.

Lifting her chin, she smiled. "Actually, I had a very productive day. Bryce even helped me." She ruffled his hair. "We deserve a night off." Glancing from one boy to the other, she said, "There's plenty of chicken fried steak left over from last night. We could make sandwiches and have a picnic."

Both boys cheered.

Tessa's suddenly shy gaze drifted to Dirk's. "Though, since we won't be working on the house, I understand if you'd prefer to go on home and have an evening to yourself."

Sadly, he'd had far too many of those.

"But I want Mr. Dirk to go." Grayson pouted.

"Me, too." Bryce's expression echoed his brother's.

Their pleas did strange things to Dirk's heart.

Smiling, he turned his attention to Tessa. "Let's do it."

So they hurried back to the house to gather what they needed, and in short order Dirk found himself standing on a wooden pier at a picturesque kidney-shaped pond somewhere on Legacy Ranch.

"Thank you for inviting me." He glanced Tessa's way as he slowly reeled in his line. "For supper, too. That was the best chicken fried steak sandwich I've ever had."

Holding her own rod, she eyed Grayson and Bryce on the bank farther down. "You're welcome. My boys can be quite insistent when they want something."

With the sun slowly descending, disappointment settled over him. Perhaps Tessa hadn't wanted him to come. Had she been hoping for some time alone with her sons?

"And I'm happy for the company." Beneath an Astros ball cap, she smiled his way. "It's nice to have another adult to converse with. One who understands the dynamics of our family. You're so patient with Grayson." She cast her line, sending it arching over the water. "That reminds me, did you tell him he'd worked enough to pay off the laser thingy?"

Dirk chuckled. She never could remember the name. "I did." He flung his own line in the opposite direction. "He wants to continue working with me."

"I suspected as much. He really enjoys spending time with you."

"And I enjoy having him around." Glancing over his shoulder, he watched as Grayson reeled in an empty hook, Molly at his side. "So does Molly."

Tessa eyed the duo. "Do you think she senses Grayson's struggles?"

Not to mention his mother's. "Absolutely. Molly is part mobility, part psychiatric service dog."

Tessa reeled in her line but didn't cast again. Instead, she walked his way. "Tell me about your life before the accident. That is, if you don't mind."

He shrugged, casting again, hoping for nonchalance when, in fact, he rarely discussed his former life. "We lived outside of Austin. I worked as an architect. A typical suburban family, I suppose. Lindsey was a stay-at-home mom, though she'd planned to return to work once Emory started kindergarten."

"Why'd you come back home?"

Gathering his thoughts, he absently turned the reel. After all Tessa had shared with him, she deserved more than a generic response. "I felt as though my life had been ripped away. Lindsey and Emory were the reason I got up every morning. Without them…"

He cleared his throat. "While I recovered at my folks', Austin became this faraway land. I couldn't imagine going back. So, I quit my job, sold our home and determined to start over." Gripping his rod, he stood it on end beside him and faced her. "Rediscovering my love for woodworking and the hands-on side of building was therapeutic. So I started taking on consignments. And after turning an old barn at our place into a home for myself, I decided to try my hand at contracting, as well."

She watched him intently. "Have you ever thought about returning to Austin?"

"No. Country life suits me just fine."

Rubbing her arms, she turned to stare out over the water. "I wish I had your courage. I've often contemplated moving to Legacy Ranch, but leaving the familiar is intimidating."

"It can be. But ask yourself where you're the happiest."

She puffed out a laugh. "That's easy. Here."

The revelation had a strange and unexpected sensation pulsing through him. One that was probably best ignored. "Well, have you ever—"

"I got one!" Across the way, Bryce struggled to reel in his catch.

His brother attempted to help as Dirk rushed toward them, Tessa on his heels.

"It's huge," Grayson grunted. "I can't—"

At the water's edge, Dirk reached for the bowed rod. "Whoa! You weren't kidding. This thing's a monster." Finally the impressive bass broke through the surface, twisting and turning.

Tessa stepped out of the way as Dirk maneuvered it onto the bank.

Suddenly, she yelped. And her wide eyes set his heart to hammering.

Her arms flailing, he reached for her, but she stumbled backward and fell into the water with a splash.

Molly barked.

"Tessa!" Abandoning the fish, Dirk followed Molly into the shallow water, his heart pounding.

Knees in the air, Tessa sat on her bottom, head down, water around her hips while her body jerked.

"Are you hurt?" He dropped beside her. "Is anything broken?" Then he realized she was laughing.

Shaking her head, she continued to guffaw. "Just call me Grace."

As his muscles relaxed, a chortle escaped his lips. Then another. When Tessa looked up at him, he laughed even harder. They both did.

"I-I'm sorry, Tessa." He tried to stifle himself but failed. "I'm not laughing at you." Tears spilled onto his cheeks. When was the last time he'd genuinely laughed?

Still amused, Tessa pushed to her feet, splashing him in the process.

He took hold of her hand and helped her onto the bank.

Meanwhile, her sons watched them as though they'd lost their minds.

But Dirk couldn't seem to stop laughing. As though it had been bottled up inside of him for so long that it had to escape. And it felt amazing.

## Chapter Six

If laughter was the best medicine, then Tessa and Dirk ought to be in good health after Wednesday evening. When was the last time she'd let loose like that? These last few years, she'd been so burdened by life's struggles that she thought happiness had packed its bags and moved on. But that night at the fishing hole, she felt more like her old self. The one she thought was gone forever.

And near as she could tell, she wasn't the only one who'd stumbled onto some much-needed joy. Dirk's spontaneous belly laugh was unlike anything she'd heard from him before. Making her long to hear it again.

The whole scenario seemed to bring a morsel of healing that was as inexplicable as it was unexpected. After all she'd been through, she'd latch on to whatever she could.

"Tessa? Yoo-hoo?" Sitting at the dining room table with Bryce in between them, Audrey—Hunt sister number three—snapped her fingers in front of Tessa's face early Saturday afternoon.

With a start, Tessa swatted her hand away. "What are you doing?"

"What am *I* doing? You're the one who zoned out." Audrey reached for her iced tea. "Where were you?"

"And what's with the goofy grin?" Kitty-corner from

Tessa, on Grayson's left, Meredith, the eldest Hunt daughter, arched a brow.

"What goofy grin?" Tessa winced at her defensive tone.

"The one you were wearing as you stared into space." Opposite Tessa, their baby sister, Kendall, offered her own commentary.

Suddenly squirming in her seat, Tessa glanced toward her aunt at the head of the table. While Dee remained silent, her cheeky grin suggested she concurred with Tessa's sisters.

Straightening, Tessa stabbed a bite of chicken salad with her fork. "I was simply enjoying the sound of us all being together again."

"And I've got oceanfront property in Arizona," Audrey deadpanned.

"Oh, you girls have no idea how much I miss this banter." Aunt Dee smiled. "This house gets awful quiet when y'all aren't around."

"So what is it you wanted to talk to us about?" Meredith turned her attention to Dee.

Using her fork, their aunt moved bits of pecan and dried cranberries around her plate, seemingly gathering her thoughts. Tessa couldn't help recalling Dee's comment about being afraid to share her dreams with her brother. Rather remarkable for a woman who never shied away from anything. Was she afraid Tessa's sisters would have a similar response?

Finally, Dee set the fork aside and looked around the table. "I'd like to make some changes to the ranch."

"What kind of changes?" Meredith narrowed her gaze.

"For starters, I'm havin' the log cabin renovated in hopes of rentin' it out to guests. I'm also thinkin'—with a little work—the old bunkhouse might make a nice getaway for families." She drew in a breath and exhaled with a huff. "I'm also thinkin' about turnin' a portion of the ranch into a retreat of sorts. A place for folks to escape the city and enjoy country life."

Meredith's brow puckered. "Why would people want to come out here?"

Tessa struggled to keep her groan to herself. Her big sister may be smart, but she could be so clueless.

"To escape the city." Tessa couldn't help herself. "We take the ranch for granted because it's always been a part of our lives. Most people don't have that, though, so we'd be providing it."

Meredith looked at their aunt. "How are you going to keep up with something like that when you've got a cattle ranch to run?"

Tessa glared at Meredith. Why did she have to be such a spoil sport? Just because she didn't have a life outside of her work as an attorney at their father's firm.

Smiling, Aunt Dee reached for Meredith's hand. "Now you sound like your daddy."

"You could always hire someone to oversee the retreat portion of the ranch," Tessa offered. "That reminds me, what were you and Dirk doing at the old barn the other day?"

"I wanted to know if it was salvageable." Releasing Meredith's hand, her aunt gave a weak smile. "Dirk says the inside is in great shape."

"Who's Dirk?" asked Audrey.

"He's the contractor I've got working on the cabin," said Dee.

"And I'm helping him." Grayson puffed his chest out.

"Good for you, Gray." Kendall ruffled his hair, making him blush.

"For the record," Dee began, "I'm not lookin' for any money from you gals. All I want is your permission to make some changes around the property. Though, any income would be split between the five of us."

"What would you do with the old barn?" Audrey sipped her tea.

"No idea." Their aunt shook her head. "But it's got that pretty little pond behind it. It's always been one of my favorite spots on the ranch."

"What if we turned it into a retreat center? You know, for churches or youth groups." Audrey set her glass down, glancing around the table.

"If you're going to do that, you may as well create a venue," said Meredith. "Why limit yourself to the occasional retreat when you could host weddings and other events year-round?"

Audrey's brown eyes went wide. "Great idea. I mean, with the ranch's proximity to both Houston and Austin, we could be looking at unlimited potential. Rustic venues are hugely popular."

"That's true, but where would we find things like caterers, florists, bands and DJs?" Meredith countered.

Kendall straightened. "I like to bake."

"You don't live here," Audrey pointed out. "I'm sure we could find some of those things in the surrounding areas. Brenham isn't that far away. We'd just need to do a little research."

Dee pushed her chair away from the table. "Look, girls, all I want is to make folks smile by creatin' a space where they can enjoy a different lifestyle. One that moves at a leisurely pace instead of rushin' through their day. And, maybe, make them smile in the process. Is that so wrong?"

"No, it's not." Tessa glared at her sisters.

"Good." Standing, Dee glanced around the table. "Besides, it's not like I'm gonna do everything at once. The cabin should be completed within the month. Then I'll talk to Dirk about the bunkhouse. Right now, though, I need to go check on a bull in the back eighty. Come on, Nash."

The dog hopped to his feet.

"Can I come?" Grayson perked up.

"Me, too?" Bryce scooted out of his chair.

"Probably just as well. Your mama and her sisters'll likely be talkin' 'bout me just as soon as I'm out the door." Dee winked over her shoulder before continuing into the kitchen. "Don't forget about dessert. Boys, y'all grab a couple of cookies for the road. Ladies, help yourself to this lemon meringue pie I made."

"Pie? Yum!" Kendall jumped out of her chair and headed into the kitchen.

"It appears Aunt Dee has made a lot of changes since Dad died." Meredith maneuvered the last of her chicken salad onto her fork. "The outside of this house looks better than ever."

"You know Dad didn't have much use for the ranch," said Tessa. "He'd have sold it in a heartbeat if Dee would've allowed him to. I don't blame her for seizing this opportunity to finally make it her own."

"Me, either." Audrey tucked her long blond hair behind one ear as their aunt's truck rolled past the window.

"What did I miss?" Kendall set the pie, plates and forks on the table.

"We were just discussing how nice the outside of the house looks," said Tessa.

"What's the story with the living room?" Meredith twisted for a better view. "Did you know there was shiplap?"

"No," said Tessa. "I'd planned to either remove the paneling and paint or paint over it until Dirk suggested there might be shiplap. Now that the wallpaper is gone, I need to remove a gazillion nails before sanding and painting. So, please, remove as many nails as you like. Because once that room is complete, I'll repeat the process in here." She motioned around the dining room.

Chin cradled in one hand, Audrey eyed her as Kendall served up the pie. "Sounds like this Dirk fellow is doing a lot more than renovating the cabin."

The insinuation in her tone had Tessa telling them about Grayson stealing from him, and the difference Dirk's influence had made in her son. "As it turns out, Dirk and I have a lot in common."

Meredith accepted a plate from Kendall. "How so?"

"He lost his wife and four-year-old daughter in a car accident five years ago."

"How horrible." Kendall passed a slice of pie to Tessa.

"I know." Picking up her fork, she nodded. "But because of that loss, he understands what the boys and I are going through." She sighed and dug into her pie. "Are still going through." When no one said anything, she looked at her sisters. "Don't take that the wrong way. I know you all are always there for me, and I love you for that."

"But he's traveled the same road you have." Meredith's understanding gaze met hers across the table. "That must be very helpful."

The eldest Hunt daughter had suffered her own share of loss at a young age. First when their mother died, then again when their father had insisted Meredith give the baby she'd carried up for adoption when she was seventeen.

Obviously sensing a need to change the topic, Audrey said, "You know, ladies, as I ponder Aunt Dee's plans, I'm starting to think there's more potential here than we realize. I mean, the possibilities are endless."

Tessa plunged her fork through the sweet meringue and tangy filling. "After all Dee has done for us, I think we should grant her free reign to do whatever she wants with the ranch. This place is her heart and soul. All she wants from us is our permission."

Audrey looked around the table. "Tessa's right. Aunt Dee has always been there for us."

"She was my rock when my world crumbled." Meredith stared at her untouched pie.

"Mine, too," said Tessa.

"Ditto," said Audrey.

"She's the only mom I really remember." Kendall had been eight when their mother passed and Dee came to live with them.

Tessa eyed her sisters. "Are we in agreement, then?"

"Yes," they responded collectively.

A knock sounded at the front door.

"I'll get it." Kendall stood and continued through the living room.

"It's probably Gentry looking for Dee," Tessa hollered after her.

"Why wouldn't he just call her?" Always the practical one, Meredith finally took a bite of her pie.

"Tessa, you have a guest," Kendall announced moments later.

Looking up, Tessa saw Dirk trailing her sister, Molly at his side. "Dirk." She scrambled out of her chair at an embarrassingly fast rate.

"Sorry to interrupt." He paused in the opening between the living and dining room. "I was cleaning out my truck and found Grayson's phone again. Thought he might be missing it."

Moving beside him, she took hold of the device, shaking her head. "The boy would lose his head if it wasn't screwed on." Heat crept up her neck when she realized all eyes were on them, accompanied by a couple of smirks. "Dirk, these are my sisters, Kendall, Meredith and Audrey." She pointed as she said their names. "This is Dirk and Molly." She gave the dog a pet.

"Pleased to meet all of you." He nodded in their direction.

"We were just talking about you, Dirk." Audrey cocked her head, her gaze darting between him and Tessa.

"Oh?" Dirk turned his inquisitive gray-blue eyes to Tessa.

Cringing, she could only imagine what he must be thinking. "Yes." She cleared her throat. "It seems Aunt Dee is considering a few more projects around the ranch."

"Oh, yeah?" He smiled, obviously clueless to her sisters' suspicions.

Standing, Audrey pulled out the chair opposite their aunt's vacated seat. "Why don't you have a seat, Dirk?" She cast Tessa a knowing look. "Tessa will fix you a slice of pie while we tell you all about it."

Dirk pulled up to the bunkhouse at Legacy Ranch late Wednesday afternoon after dropping Grayson off at the main house. Something the kid was rather put out about. He'd begged and pleaded to go with Dirk, but until he could be certain the structure was sound and posed no threats, Dirk wasn't going to risk it. If something happened to Grayson, Tessa would have Dirk's head.

Smiling, he emerged from his truck into the shade of a post oak and waited for Molly to bound out after him. This had been quite a week. One filled with the unexpected. Starting with an impromptu fishing expedition that left him feeling lighter than he had in years and ending with the possibility of a huge boost to his business.

But before that could happen, he needed to inspect the bunkhouse, take some measurements and get a better feel for the place Ms. D'Lynn and her nieces had introduced him to over the weekend. The building had been neglected for quite a while, though, so he wasn't about to put Grayson at risk, no matter how much the kid begged. Once Dirk was satisfied things were safe, he'd allow the boy to tag along.

A gentle breeze carried the scent of fresh air and sunshine and raised the hair on his arms as he studied the whitewashed, single-story cottonwood-board structure with a rusted metal roof and a porch that spanned its lengthy facade. With the plumbing and electrical finished at the cabin, and the mini split air conditioning and heat pump unit scheduled to go in tomorrow, the place would be complete in a couple of weeks. And while he had a few projects he'd need to see to after that, the prospect of breathing new life into another forsaken building here at Legacy Ranch energized him. God had blessed him with a knack for seeing the potential in buildings most people would consider beyond help. And he hoped that Ms. D'Lynn would decide to do something with the barn, too.

After clipping the handle to Molly's vest, they continued toward the crude structure and climbed the two steps.

"You ready for some more exploring, Molly?" Using the key Ms. D'Lynn had given him, he unlocked the padlock and tugged it free before tossing the hasp aside and pushing the flimsy door open. The same musty odor that had greeted them Saturday wafted from inside, energizing him. He loved old buildings. Their character as well as their nod to simpler times.

He looked down to find Molly staring up at him, awaiting instruction. "Heel, girl." Given his uncertainty about the integrity of the structure, he wanted Molly at his side.

The wooden floorboards creaked as they stepped inside the uninsulated, one-room structure with four small windows—two on each end—that offered limited light.

Metal bunkbeds topped with thin feather mattresses covered in blue-striped ticking stretched across the back wall, while two rough-hewn tables with crude benches sat askew on either side of the door.

He lifted the lid on a sizeable enameled pot resting atop the large, antiquated woodstove that would've been used for both heating and cooking. Not exactly practical in the searing Texas summers, yet it stood in the center of the space, its chimney stretching beyond the exposed rafters and through the roof.

When they were here Saturday, Ms. D'Lynn had shared her thoughts, which included bringing running water and electricity to the structure and adding a bathroom, a bedroom, a kitchenette and more windows. Not to mention heating and cooling. Now it was up to him to determine the most logical—and cost-effective—way to achieve that.

The sound of an engine reached his ears and had him looking out the door as Tessa brought the utility vehicle to a stop beside his truck and killed the motor. She stepped out and started toward the bunkhouse. Her hair was pulled back, and she wore an oversize T-shirt and faded denim shorts over dusty cowboy boots.

He couldn't help smiling as his mind again drifted back to that night at the fishing hole. Something had happened there. Something special and unexpected. As he laughed like he hadn't in ages, he felt alive for the first time since the accident. With most people—even his family—he often pretended he was okay, even when he wasn't. But with Tessa, he could be real, good or bad. And knowing that was strangely cathartic.

"What are you doing here? Where are the boys?"

She climbed the steps and tentatively stepped inside, her gaze darting about the space. "They're at the house with Aunt Dee. I needed a break. I think I've pulled no less than 300,229 nails today."

He felt the corners of his mouth lift. "You were counting, huh?"

She looked his way. "Of course."

"At least you're that much closer to finishing. And I'll even help you remove some more."

"I welcome any assistance. However, it would only be fair that I feed you supper, then. Aunt Dee is making her famous homemade pizza tonight."

"Sounds delicious."

"It is. She cooks it on the grill." Slipping her hands into her back pockets, she looked around. "Grayson said you were coming over here, so I thought I'd come by and see if you needed any help. You know, like someone to hold a tape measure."

"I thought I told you I bought a new laser measure." Matter of fact, he knew he had. "Even so, I know my way around a tape measure."

Narrowing her gaze, she crossed her arms. "Okay, so maybe curiosity got the best of me. That, and I'm too chicken to come over here by myself." Her gaze fell to the floor. "Stupid raccoons."

"Raccoons?" As she told him the story of her childhood encounter with a mama raccoon, he couldn't help chuckling.

"Ah, well, if we come across any vicious critters, I promise to protect you."

*The way you protected Lindsey and Emory?*

The unwanted thought blazed through his mind, twisting his gut. Somehow, he managed to dismiss it as Tessa whisked past him.

"So what are you thinking as far as dividing this one room into an inviting getaway?" Stopping near the far windows, she faced him.

"Um, well, off the top of my head, I'm considering a bedroom at one end to give mom and dad some privacy."

"Good idea." She nodded.

"Then a bathroom next to that."

Another nod. "Kitchen?"

"Right there." He gestured to the wall behind the bunk beds. "Single-wall layout, opposite the front door, leaving room for a table and chairs here." He pointed to the area around the stove. "And I'll probably add a window over the kitchen."

Looking around, she nodded. "We definitely need more windows in here."

*We?* That one little word stirred his curiosity, along with something else he quickly sent packing.

"By putting the bed, bath and kitchen in that two-thirds," she continued, "you'll have space for a sitting area." Her brow puckered as she faced him. "Or combo sitting/sleeping. Where were you planning to have the kids sleep?"

"I'm still trying to determine the logistics of that. What are your thoughts on a foldout bed?"

"Like a sofa sleeper?"

"Yeah."

"That's rather limiting. I mean, what if they have more than two kids?"

He eyed the back wall where he'd contemplated adding another window. "What about bunk beds, or a Murphy bed? Perhaps one on both the front and rear wall. Twin size." Turning, he noticed her glancing toward the rafters.

Arms crossed, she tapped a finger against her lips. "Do you suppose there's room for a loft?"

He followed her gaze. "Possibly. We'll be adding insulation, so that will drop the ceiling some."

She faced him now. "Even if the beds were nothing more than mattresses on the floor, kids would be tickled pink. They love stuff like that. Especially in a setting like this that may be as close to camping as some will ever get." Smiling, she lifted a shoulder. "Adventurous adults might think it's cool, too."

"I never considered a loft, but it's not a bad idea. We could put a stairway along this back wall. Then there'd be room for a sofa sleeper or such down here, for seating, or in case someone needs an extra bed."

"Exactly. So it could easily sleep, say, as many as ten people."

"Well, it is a bunkhouse." Excitement coursing through his veins, he said, "I'll incorporate that into the design as well as one without, then Ms. D'Lynn can determine which she likes the best." He looked at Tessa. "Where'd you come up with such great ideas?"

Wrinkling her nose, she said, "I may or may not have a slight addiction to home improvement shows."

"Have you made many improvements at your house?"

She shook her head. "Not a one. I just tuck them away in here." She tapped the side of her head.

"Well, they certainly came in handy today."

"It's about time. It's getting kind of crowded in there."

"Then I'll have to pick your brain more often."

"Please do. I'd much rather see those ideas in person than just dreaming about them."

"I use a computer design program, so once I get it ready, I'll be able to show you how your ideas come together."

"That's cool. Especially since the boys and I will probably be gone by the time you start the project."

The reminder pricked his heart. He would miss having Grayson around. Not to mention the woman who got him like no one else.

"We'll just have to visit on occasion so we can see the progress."

True. Houston wasn't that far away. Still, things wouldn't be the same.

# Chapter Seven

Wayward strands of Tessa's hair whipped around her face as she drove back to the ranch house, all the while her insides were doing a happy dance. Not because of Aunt Dee's pizza night or Dirk's offer to help her remove nails from the shiplap. Nope, this was all about the bunkhouse.

Though she couldn't recall ever having spent any time there, the thought of transforming it into something new that people could actually enjoy had all sorts of ideas playing through her mind. How she wished she could be here to help with its overhaul. Sadly, she'd likely be back in school before any real work even began on the place.

That didn't mean she couldn't give some input, though. Assuming Dirk didn't mind. Then again, he had asked her opinion. Still, she shouldn't bombard him. At least not until she'd narrowed her plethora of ideas down to some practical ones that made sense for the bunkhouse.

Her stomach growled as the ranch house came into view. The boys weren't the only ones looking forward to Aunt Dee's pizza. And then it would be back to the nails. Thankfully, she only had one more section to tackle. With Dirk's help, they might even finish tonight. Then she'd have to fill the holes before giving the walls a good sanding. She'd obviously had no idea what she was getting herself into when she'd started this project. After all, on television, the process only took an hour.

Once it was done, though, the living and dining rooms would look completely different. Of that she was certain. However, she doubted she'd have both spaces completed in time for Aunt Dee's annual July Fourth celebration, so she needed to keep that in mind.

After parking under the live oak, she strolled up the drive to the carriage porch. When she pushed the door open, the spicy scent of Dee's homemade sauce captivated her senses.

She kicked off her boots before continuing into the kitchen, where Dee stood at the old butcher-block island, Bryce on a stool beside her, licking his lips as he watched his aunt sprinkle her special cheese blend over the super-size pizza.

A sigh escaped as Tessa approached them. "It smells divine in here."

"First pizza's already on the grill."

Tessa jolted from her aroma-induced coma. "That reminds me, I hope you don't mind, but I invited Dirk for supper. He offered to help me remove nails tonight, so I felt like I should repay him somehow."

"Not to worry, sister. I made plenty."

"She's makin' me and Grayson a super-duper cheesy pizza." Bryce's toothless grin was on full display.

"I can see that."

"And after supper, Aunt Dee's gonna let me and Grayson go in the hillbilly hot tub while she tends her garden."

The hillbilly hot tub was an eight-foot-wide, round galvanized stock tank that served as a pool. It was where both of her boys had learned to swim and put their faces in the water. And while they were too big to actually swim in it anymore, it was still a fun way to cool off.

"Wow. You've got quite the night ahead of you." How she loved the simplicity of country life.

Glancing from the kitchen into the family room, she said, "Where's your brother?"

Her youngest shrugged. "Upstairs, I think."

Meanwhile, Nash was parked between Dee and Bryce, his nose in the air as he waited patiently for something to drop his way.

"In that case, I'm going to run up and check on them. Dirk will be here shortly. He had a couple more things he wanted to inspect at the bunkhouse."

"Not a problem." Dee remained focused on her masterpiece. "We'll be here."

Tessa made her way through the entry hall, pausing to admire the living room as she reached the stairs. Despite being a work in progress, the space already looked better. Definitely brighter. And it would be even more so once it was painted. If she could just decide on a color.

Speaking of colors, what would they do with the bunkhouse? Currently, it was beyond rustic with all that dark exposed wood. Once it was insulated, though, they'd have to decide whether to use Sheetrock or do something else. But what?

She'd have to ask Dirk about cost-effective options.

Upstairs, she continued toward the back of the house and the room she now only shared with her boys when her sisters were here. Aunt Dee had suggested that, since the boys were getting older, Tessa should use one of the other three rooms the rest of the time, and she was more than happy to do so.

Noting how quiet it was, Tessa wondered if Grayson had fallen asleep. He'd been a real trooper about getting up early every weekday.

She peered around the corner to see him lying on the top bunk. Assuming he was asleep, she started to leave.

Then she heard a sniffle.

Was Grayson crying? She continued into the space. "Gray, what's wrong?"

Grayson hastily wiped his eyes with the back of his hands as she approached. "Nothing." He sniffed.

"Are you feeling okay? You're not coming down with something, are you?" Using the bottom bunk to boost her, she reached over the rail and touched a hand to his brow.

"I'm fine." He jerked away, his defiance on full display.

With a deep breath, she willed herself to remain unaffected. "Mr. Dirk is going to join us for supper. Then he's going to help me remove more nails." She wanted to brush the hair away from his face but decided against it. "You're welcome to help, if you'd like."

"That's boring."

She'd expected such a response. "That's alright. You've already put in a full day's work. You're allowed to do something fun. I hear Aunt Dee says you and Bryce can cool off in the hillbilly hot tub."

"Yeah." He had yet to look at her. And she was struggling to determine what had him in such a foul mood. Had he and Dirk had a falling out? But then, wouldn't Dirk have mentioned something to her at the bunkhouse?

"Gigi called me."

Tessa cringed a little. Had her mother-in-law said something to upset him? Nick had been her in-laws' only child. And his mother, Gina, had deeply grieved the loss of her son. Depression had her withdrawing, and she lost a lot of weight that first year after his death. She even grew anxious when she didn't hear from Tessa or the boys. And Dan, her sweet husband, struggled to keep his wife afloat, all while working through his own grief. Thankfully, he'd finally convinced Gina to see a Christian counselor, and the woman had made great strides this past year.

"What did she have to say?"

Grayson shrugged. "She misses me and Bryce. Wanted to know when we're coming home."

Could that be why Grayson had been so contrary about spending the entire summer at the ranch? Had her mother-in-law mentioned something while he and Bryce were with them that last weekend before they left?

Not that Tessa had any intention of altering her plans. Though, perhaps, she could offer a compromise. "What if we invited Gigi and Pops to come out here for Aunt Dee's Fourth of July celebration? Would you like that?" If the cabin was finished, perhaps they could stay there. She'd need to run that past Aunt Dee, though. Then again, Independence Day was only three weeks from tomorrow, so even if Dirk had completed his work, the place likely wouldn't be ready for guests.

Grayson sat up. "I guess."

Tessa heard a knock at the front door.

"That's probably Mr. Dirk." She stepped down to the floor. "Are you ready for some of Aunt Dee's pizza?"

Nodding, he climbed off of the bed before bounding down the stairs.

Tessa watched after him, relieved Grayson wasn't sick. However, she couldn't shake the feeling that something was troubling him. While Dirk had definitely been a good influence, Grayson still had a long way to go. Much longer than their summer break, she was afraid.

Just after five Friday afternoon, Dirk hastily stashed containers of lettuce leaves, tomatoes, potato salad and guacamole into his refrigerator. He rarely had company. When he did, it was only members of his own family. Even then, he'd never prepared a meal for any of them, unless you counted the microwave popcorn and ice cream sundaes he'd made for his niece and nephew when they joined him for a movie night while their parents and Dirk's folks attended Christmas parties on the same night last year. So why he'd offered to fix supper for Tessa, her boys and her aunt was still a mystery.

So he'd knocked off work early today so he could make a run to the grocery store in Brenham. Closing the fridge, he eyed the buns, tortilla chips, salsa and three different desserts spread across the island that also served as a dining table. He still had to shower and get the hamburger patties made. He'd told Tessa to arrive at six, so to say he was feeling overwhelmed would be the understatement of the century.

As he and Tessa pulled the last of the nails from the shiplap Wednesday night, the topic of the barn had come up, along with the various ideas Tessa's sisters had tossed about for its use. Yet Tessa couldn't seem to wrap her mind around the concept of creating a viable space inside the old barn at Legacy Ranch. "How is that even possible?" she'd asked, throwing up her hands.

Of course, Dirk had a perfect example for her, so he'd suggested she, Ms. D'Lynn and the boys come over and take a look at his place. Then the next thing he knew, he'd offered to feed them, as well. Words like "We'll make a night of it" had never come out of his mouth before. So where they'd come from that night, he had no idea. And he'd been scrambling ever since to come up with something more than the ready-made meals he usually had stocked in his fridge.

Even though Ms. D'Lynn had graciously bowed out, he still had to feed Tessa, Grayson and Bryce without coming across as completely inept. Thankfully, he knew how to grill.

Lindsey had even dubbed him The Grill Master. But that was back when they used to invite friends over on a regular basis. Those days were long gone.

Returning to the refrigerator, he pulled the door open and reached for the ground sirloin, a hopeful Molly watching his every move. Until a knock sounded at the door.

Oh, no. They were early.

His stomach churning, he glanced over his shoulder and out the window to see his brother's pickup in the driveway. "Door's open," he hollered as he closed the refrigerator.

Jared strolled into the succinct open space that was home to both the kitchen and living areas. "You're home early." Making his way around one of the barn's original hand-hewn posts, he caught sight of the food and empty sacks littering the island. "What's with all the groceries? You havin' a party and forgot to invite me?"

Dirk set the meat beside the sink on the island and washed his hands. "Yeah, because I'm such a party guy." He grabbed a towel and dried his hands.

His brother momentarily removed his filthy Ariat ball cap to scratch his head. "Then what gives?"

Telling Jared that Tessa and her boys were coming for supper was apt to have his brother reading way too much into an otherwise innocent event. But then, with his brother living on the same property, it would be just like him to come back later to see what was happening. Like the time he spied on a thirteen-year-old Dirk and his best friend when they'd come to this same barn to smoke a cigarette his friend had lifted off his dad. Then ran home and told their parents.

Dirk retrieved a sheet pan from the cupboard behind him and set it on the counter before tearing open the package of meat. "Ms. D'Lynn—the woman I've been working for—

is thinking about doing something with an old barn on her property."

"Like what?"

Dirk shrugged as he grabbed a handful of ground beef. "Her nieces have tossed out countless ideas, one of which was a venue, but she has yet to nail anything down."

"That's cool." Jared rounded the island to grab a glass from the cupboard. "But what does that have to do with all this food?" Now beside Dirk, he filled his cup at the sink. "You thinking about going into the catering business?"

"Very funny." He set the first patty on the pan. "Her niece and great-nephews are in for the summer. Tessa— Ms. D'Lynn's niece—can't seem to visualize the barn beyond the dilapidated state it's currently in. So I invited her and her boys to take a look at my place."

The corners of Jared's mouth twitched, mischief glinting in his eyes. "Is she pretty?"

"What's that got to do with anything?" Dirk could only hope his brother missed the defensiveness in his tone.

"You're right. With two kids I guess that means there's a husband in the mix." He gulped his water while Dirk worked on the next burger.

"No, she's a widow." Dirk cringed as soon as the words left his mouth. Why had he said that out loud?

Jared's smile grew wide. "And you're preparing supper for them?"

Dirk squeezed the meat in his hand, causing it to ooze between his fingers. "Look, I don't have time for twenty questions. Tessa's nine-year-old son has been working with me at the cabin. He's still trying to make sense of his father's death, and that's led to some trouble at school, so I'm trying to help him. As for me and Tessa, we both lost our spouses, so we get each other on a level most people can't understand. But there's nothing romantic, alright?"

"Okay, bro." Hands in the air, Jared took a step back. "Take it easy. I'll get out of your hair."

"Thank you."

"You're welcome." Jared opened the plastic container of brownie bites and grabbed a couple, immediately popping one in his mouth.

"What're you doing?"

"Just tiding myself over till Hannah has supper ready." A speck of brownie followed the words coming out of his mouth.

"You're disgusting." Dirk turned his attention back to the meat. "Now get out of here before you make a mess."

With Jared gone and the patties finished, Dirk put the tray in the refrigerator then rushed to his bedroom for a quick shower and change of clothes. Leaving him just enough time to start the grill and locate bowls for the chips, salsa and guacamole.

With the appetizers ready, he perched his hands on his hips and took in the space he'd vacuumed and dusted before going to the cabin this morning. "I think we're ready, Molly."

Just then, movement outside the window caught his attention and he spotted Tessa's SUV coming up the gravel drive.

"And just in the nick of time." He went to the front door, followed by a vestless Molly, and stepped outside to greet their guests. The evening air was pleasant, mid-eighties, with low humidity. Yet that didn't stop him from breaking into a sweat when Tessa stepped out of her vehicle looking very feminine in a floral sundress.

"This does *not* look like a barn." Tossing her door closed, she stared at the structure that now boasted metal siding as well as the roof. "At least not an old one. I mean, it's not even made of wood."

Hands in the pockets of his shorts, he ambled across the grass while Molly beelined for the boys, her tail wagging. "That's one of the nice things about old barns." He met Tessa's gaze. "They look just as at home in a modern setting as they do something rustic." Needing a distraction from the delightful fragrance emanating from her, he turned his attention to the boys. "Hey, guys. You hungry?"

"Uh-huh." Bryce gave a nod.

Meanwhile, Grayson hugged Molly, burying his face in her neck. Something he did often. Dirk's canine friend had been clinging to Grayson more, too. The boy had been behaving differently these last few days. More withdrawn. As though something was bothering him. Yet whenever Dirk said anything, the kid insisted he was fine.

"Let's go inside. You boys can help yourself to some chips while I prove to your mom that my house really is an old barn."

"Dirk, this looks so modern." Tessa's gaze roamed the structure as they continued up the walk.

"That was by design. The medium brown metal siding paired with the darker metal roof gives the illusion that it's a new structure." He reached for the door. "And then when you step inside..." Swinging the door wide, he motioned for them to enter.

The boys gave a collective "whoa" as their gazes moved up, down and all around, taking in the hand-hewn posts, beams and braces that stretched toward the exposed rafters.

Seemingly speechless, Tessa stood there, mouth agape as she looked around. "You did this all by yourself?"

"Most of it, yes." He'd needed to challenge himself. And

while it hadn't been easy, it had given him the confidence he'd needed to start his own business.

He retrieved the framed photo collage from one of two live-edge side tables situated at each end of the leather sofa. "This is what it used to look like."

Her gaze darted between the images of the once-dilapidated wood structure and the finished product. "The transformation. This is amazing. You were right, about the guts of the structure adding character. It's modern, yet still feels cozy."

"Would you like a tour?"

"Yes, please."

"It's fairly straightforward." Returning the photos to the table, he said, "This is the living room."

"I like these stained concrete floors." Tessa dragged the toe of her sandal over the smooth surface colored to look like rustic fieldstone. "Attractive while playing into the industrial vibe you've kinda got going on."

"You noticed."

"Chalk it up to all those home improvement shows." Her wink had his heart racing.

"The kitchen's right over there." He pointed to the opposite end of the space.

"Where's your bedroom?" Bryce peered up at him.

Smiling, Dirk said, "See those barn doors?" He pointed to the wall along the other side of the living room. When Bryce nodded, Dirk said, "Go ahead and open them."

While Bryce grabbed the handle on one of the rustic wood doors with frosted glass inserts, Grayson hurried to take hold of the other. Then they opened them to reveal a queen-size bed and a wall of windows that overlooked the cattle-dotted pasture.

"Oh, wow." The appreciation in Tessa's voice had Dirk standing a little taller. "That is beautiful."

"It has a full bath off the side there." Turning to look down the hallway, he added, "Then there's a half bath across from the kitchen, and my shop is just down that hall on the other side of the barn."

"Can we see it?" For the first time since they got here, Grayson seemed excited.

"Sure."

While the boys took off down the hall with Molly, Tessa remained beside him, moving at a more leisurely pace. "Thank you for inviting us tonight. In only a matter of minutes you have opened my eyes. Now I'm starting to envision the potential for the barn at Legacy Ranch." Her sweet fragrance wrapped around him, sending his mind down a trail it had no business venturing.

"Believe it or not, you and the boys are the first people outside of my family to see this place." He cringed as soon as the words spilled out. He must sound pathetic.

Her steps halted as she looked up at him. "Are you serious? How long have you lived here?"

"A little over two years." Shoving his hands into his pockets, he longed for a rock to crawl under. "I guess I've become a bit of a hermit."

She continued to watch him, her scent wrapping around him, making it difficult to look away. Yet instead of the sympathy he expected to see, he saw only understanding. "Trust me, if it weren't for those two—" she nodded toward her boys "—I would be, too."

Staring into her beautiful eyes, he found himself longing to come out of hiding and truly live again. But to what end? Tessa would be leaving in August, and he'd find himself alone once more.

Then again, Houston wasn't that far away.

# Chapter Eight

The last thing Tessa wanted to be reminded of Sunday was that it was Father's Day. One of those greeting card holidays that rang hollow for her now that her husband and father were gone. But that hadn't stopped the church from recognizing all of the fathers and grandfathers, and then the pastor's message was all about being a godly father.

So now that they were home, she was determined to change the subject.

Once they'd finished lunch, she said, "You boys go change into your swimsuits. Be sure to wear a sun shirt, too, so you don't get sunburned." She'd promised the boys a day at the swimming hole in hopes of distracting them from the so-called holiday.

While they got ready, she willed herself to concentrate on gathering snacks and drinks. Her mind had been awhirl since visiting Dirk's place. Seeing what he'd done with that old barn had gotten her creative juices flowing. The evening had also given her some valuable insight into the man himself.

His food choices had revealed he was conscientious, opting for a simple entree like hamburgers, knowing the boys would like them, but then offering brioche buns in addition to the standard white eight-pack variety. And while her sons were delighted to have vanilla ice cream and chocolate syrup

Mindy Obenhaus                          105

with their brownie bites, she found the salted caramel gelato
was a much better pairing.

The decor in his home suggested Dirk was practical yet
sentimental, with items like the rustic console table he'd built
from the barn's original aged wood siding. Situated prominently behind the sofa that faced a wall of windows overlooking the pasture, it wasn't so much the table as it was the
items atop it that revealed what he valued most—a well-used
Bible and family photos.

Two five-by-seven images of Dirk's little girl had sat
alongside an eight-by-ten of him, his wife and their precious child. Tessa had never seen him smile the way he had
in that photo. So big, so bright that his gray-blue eyes sparkled. His family had been his world. And then that world
was shattered. She couldn't help wondering how he was feeling this Father's Day.

She'd actually invited him to join them today, thinking
he, too, might welcome the distraction, but he hadn't seemed
interested. Then again, his father was still alive, so perhaps
his family had plans. Or he simply wanted to be alone.

Just the thought of that made her sad.

"Tessa, hon." Her aunt came into the kitchen. "I heard
something at church today I thought I'd pass along to you,
in case you were interested."

"What's that?" Halting her mission, Tessa brushed her
hair away from her face.

"Seems they're lookin' for a second-grade teacher at the
elementary school in Hope Crossing." Her aunt lifted a brow.
"I know how much you like it out here. The boys, too. So,
I thought I'd mention it in case you wanted to look into it."

Tessa simply stared. Only in her wildest dreams had she
dreamed of calling Legacy Ranch home. Wishful thinking,
so to speak, because the turnover rate in small districts like

Hope Crossing that only had one elementary, one middle and one high school was low.

Then she thought of her boys and how much they enjoyed their summers out here. But how would living here permanently impact them? Grayson, in particular.

"Wow. Yeah, that is something worth considering." She grabbed a bag of mini carrots from the counter and added them to the cooler.

"I know movin' out here would be a big change. Course you and the boys would be welcome to live here with me, if you like."

Talk about sweetening the deal. Living with or near her aunt would be a dream come true for her. But what about Grayson and Bryce?

"I appreciate that. But I'm going to have to think—and pray—on this for a bit."

"I understand. They'll be acceptin' applicants through the end of the month." Dee paused. "Change the subject, how long do you plan on swimmin'?"

"Not a clue." Tessa added a bag of grapes to the cooler and closed the lid. "Depends how quickly the boys wear out. Why?"

"Oh, Gentry mentioned takin' me to some shop in Brenham. Said it might have some interestin' pieces for the log cabin."

Seemed they were both excited about all the projects around the ranch. Dee had been asking for Tessa's input on everything from cabinet finishes to appliances, fixtures and furniture for the cabin. *Yet another reason for you to move out here.*

She shook the thought away. "How late are they open?"

Her aunt shrugged. "Four. Maybe five."

"Oh." It was close to one now. However, since Gentry

had asked her… "That's alright, though. You go ahead and go. We'll be fine."

Her aunt squared her shoulders. "Now, don't go placating me, missy. I said I'd go swimmin', and I'm a woman of my word. I'll just ask Gentry where it is and take myself sometime."

Tessa's phone rang. Eyeing it on the counter, she saw Dirk's name. She picked it up, tapping the screen before setting the device to her ear. "Hey, how's it going?"

"Not too bad. Kind of boring, though. Is it too late for me to join you and the boys for some swimming?"

For whatever reason, her heart took flight. "Sure. We're in the process of getting ready now." Her cheeks heated as her aunt sent her a knowing grin.

"In that case, I'll get there as quick as I can."

"We'll see you soon." Ending the call, she bit her bottom lip as an uncharacteristic burst of excitement bubbled inside of her.

"Let me guess." Dee strolled toward her. "Dirk's gonna join you."

"Yes, ma'am, he is." Ignoring her aunt's impish grin, Tessa straightened. "Guess you're free to join Gentry and shop till your little heart's content. That is, unless you still want to go with us."

Her aunt wrinkled her nose. "Do you think the boys'll be disappointed?"

"Devastated."

"Really?" Dee winced.

"I'm kidding. But if it'll make you feel better, go ask them."

"I'll do that now." The woman smiled as she headed into the hall. "Maybe I'll offer to bring them back a treat."

Tessa chuckled as the woman continued upstairs, then

filled an insulated beverage dispenser with water before hurrying to change into her swimsuit. Topping it with a tank-style dress, she shoved her feet into a pair of flip-flops and gathered towels for everyone before heading downstairs as someone knocked on the door.

Assuming it was Dirk, she said, "Grayson, will you get that for me?" After learning on their way home from church that Dirk would not be joining them, her son's attitude had become a little surly so she hoped this would improve it.

Thankfully, she was right. And by the time they pulled the utility vehicle up to the secluded oasis, Grayson was in better spirits. Of course, it helped that Molly was clinging to him. Something Tessa still had her suspicions about.

She brought the vehicle to a stop in the shade of a sprawling live oak, where a nearby picnic table provided a dry place for towels and food, while a thirty-foot pier jutted over the spring-fed waters, allowing them to jump into its deepest section.

After Dirk helped her unload their gear, Tessa tossed her cover-up on the table alongside the cooler and followed the guys across the pier until it came to a tee in the bright sunshine.

Grayson dropped the round inner tube float on the deck. "Last one in is a rotten egg."

"That'll probably be me." With Molly at his side, Dirk sat down on the built-in bench and proceeded to remove his prosthetic.

Tessa couldn't help but stare, right along with her sons.

Until Dirk caught her watching.

While he smiled, she looked away, her cheeks heating as though she'd intruded on something private. "I-I'm sorry. Guess I'm a little curious."

"Don't be sorry. Unless you live with an amputee, it's not something people see every day."

"It comes off?" Bryce stared wide-eyed.

Tessa found herself chuckling along with Dirk.

"Of course." Dirk set the artificial limb aside, along with his towel. "Wearing it in the water wouldn't be good for it. Besides, I don't need it in the water."

"How come?" Grayson stared as Dirk peeled small socks from his stump.

"I can kick my legs—what's left of them, anyway—just like you." After setting his things aside, he removed his T-shirt before standing. "Let's go." With Molly flanking him, he hopped to the edge of the pier, and before Tessa knew what was happening, she and Molly were being pelted with water droplets as all three males hit the water.

Dirk looked up at her from the clear water, his muscular arms moving back and forth. "This is definitely refreshing. You planning to join us?"

Before she could second-guess herself, she cannonballed into the water. When she surfaced, she saw Molly pacing back and forth on the pier, as though she was a lifeguard ready to jump in the instant her assistance was needed.

Tessa had no idea how long they played in the cool water, nor did she care. How could she when they were all smiling. Even Grayson appeared to be having the time of his life. And that had her thinking about the teaching position Dee mentioned. If they lived here, she and the boys could do things like this all the time. Of course, there'd still be the day-to-day routines, but to have the option of slipping away to this and other fun spots around the ranch whenever they wanted, if only for a short time—definitely enticing. Not to mention being with Aunt Dee.

When the boys complained they were hungry, they all returned to the picnic table along the bank for snacks.

While they munched on grapes, chunks of cantaloupe and string cheese, Tessa checked her phone in case Aunt Dee had tried to call. While there was nothing from her aunt, there was a text from Gina reminding her to have the boys call Dan to wish him a happy Father's Day.

Tessa cringed. She'd been so busy shunning the so-called holiday, she'd forgotten about the boys' other grandfather.

"Boys, you need to call Pops and wish him a happy Father's Day."

"Now?" Grayson frowned. "But we're having fun."

"If you don't do it now, I'm afraid we'll forget."

"It's okay, Grayson." Bryce rolled a grape between his fingers. "It won't take that long."

Her eldest son's shoulders dropped as though an invisible weight pressed down on him. "I didn't bring my phone."

"You can use mine." She slid hers across the table.

"Fine." Taking hold of the phone, he stood and walked away.

"Wait for me." Bryce took off after him.

She watched them go with a sigh.

"Problem?" Holding a handful of grapes, Dirk eyed her across the table.

"More like a knee-jerk reaction." She shifted her attention from the boys to Dirk. "Nick was my in-laws' only child. So they were devastated when he passed." She sucked in a breath, not wanting to paint Dan and Gina in a bad light. Grief had a way of bringing out the worst in the otherwise best people. "Let's just say it's taken me a while to find a new norm with them."

"I can completely relate."

Without thinking, she reached for his hand. "Thank you for saying that. It's nice to know someone understands."

Their eyes met, and she withdrew her hand, suddenly embarrassed by the brazen move.

Then she saw Bryce coming toward them. "Back already?"

Her youngest nodded. "I told Pops happy Father's Day, just like you said." He snagged another grape. "Can I go back in the water now?"

"Let's wait for Grayson."

He looked up at Dirk. "I made a new friend at church today."

"Oh, yeah? What's his name?"

"Owen. And I'm gonna go play at his house."

As Dirk glanced her way, Tessa said, "His dad used to work for Aunt Dee, and it turns out they live just up the road, so Owen's mom invited him to come over and play with Owen sometime." She looked at her son now. "But we haven't made any plans yet."

A few minutes later, Grayson trudged toward them.

"Come on, Grayson. Let's swim some more," said Bryce.

Dropping on the bench beside Molly, Grayson hugged the dog's neck. "You can go."

Tessa couldn't believe he wasn't interested. "What did Pops and Gigi have to say?"

He shrugged. "They're going out to eat with some friends."

"I'm sure they'll enjoy that." She was thankful her mother-in-law was getting out again. "You didn't happen to mention the Fourth of July, did you?" Though Dee was fine with having them come, Tessa had yet to contact them.

He shook his head as Molly rested her chin in his lap.

"I'll call them this week, then." She glanced at Bryce eagerly waiting nearby. "Grayson, are you sure you don't want to swim?"

He shook his head.

"Okay." She stood, glancing at her watch. "Feel free to join us whenever you're ready."

Over the next twenty minutes she checked on him twice. By then, Bryce was starting to get bored without his brother, despite her and Dirk's efforts to keep him entertained.

And Tessa was growing frustrated.

Returning to the picnic table, she said, "Are you feeling alright, Grayson? Maybe you got too much sun."

"I'm *fine*." Elbows on the table, he dropped his head in his hand.

He may be fine, however his attitude was anything but.

Still, she willed herself to remain unaffected. "In that case, we'll plan to be out of the water in fifteen minutes and then go on back to the house. So if you want to swim, I suggest you do it now before time runs out."

Yet despite giving him countdown warnings, he didn't join them until they were getting out of the water.

"Aww, I was about to get in," he said as Bryce climbed the ladder to join him on the pier.

"I'm sorry, Grayson," she said. "You had plenty of warning."

He frowned, his bottom lip pooching out. "You just don't want me to swim with you."

"You know that's not true." She glanced Dirk's way as Molly waited for him to exit the water.

"Yes, it is. You don't want me around. Just like you didn't want Dad around."

The verbal slap had Tessa's eyes widening.

"Grayson—" Dirk's voice was low and held a calm she did not possess at the moment "—that's no way to talk to your mother."

"She hates me. Just like she hated my dad."

Tessa struggled to breathe. Her worst nightmare was coming true. She'd lost her husband, now she was losing her son. And she couldn't seem to help Grayson any more than she could Nick.

Dirk had gone home shortly after they returned to Ms. D'Lynn's. Though it wasn't what he'd wanted. Tessa was hurting, and he'd longed to stay and offer whatever comfort he could. Yet she'd insisted he'd be better off at his place where he wasn't surrounded by a bunch of wet blankets. Little did she know, wet blankets or not, he'd come to care for her and her sons a great deal. So it didn't matter where he was—if they hurt, he hurt. And what he'd witnessed at the swimming hole broke his heart.

Back at his place, he'd done the only thing he knew to do. Pray. Although it had been more like pleading as he'd asked God to bring healing to that family. In the brief time he'd known Tessa and her boys, they'd brought something to his life that had been missing for far too long. As though his heart had started beating again. Making him even more grateful for the additional work at Legacy Ranch that would afford him more time with them.

Still, it hurt him to see Grayson so somber this Monday morning. He wasn't usually that way. But this last week or so he'd changed. Molly had been clinging to the kid, too. And Dirk wished he could figure out why.

Until that happened, though, he had to keep moving forward. On both the cabin and in his relationship with Grayson. Proving himself to be a safe haven where Grayson would feel comfortable and, Lord willing, open up about what had him so troubled.

Today they were installing the kitchen cabinets he'd built out of reclaimed wood that would feel right at home in the rustic cabin. Since it was a small galley kitchen, there were only two and a half uppers, four lowers and a sink base, so the installation shouldn't take too long.

Grayson was a good right-hand man. He'd learned the names of all of the tools and what they were used for. So while Dirk worked on the first upper, Grayson stood nearby, ready to hand Dirk whichever tool he requested. They made a good team. Dirk just wished the kid was in a better mood.

"You know—" Dirk stepped down off the ladder after attaching the first upper "—those were some pretty harsh words you said about your mom yesterday. I may not have known her for very long, but I can say with great certainty that she does *not* hate you."

The boy's gaze fell. "I was mad."

"That doesn't make it right. What were you mad about? I mean, you seemed to be having a great time." Until he talked with his grandparents. Could they have said something that upset him? Though Dirk couldn't imagine what that might be.

With one hand atop Molly, who stood at his side, Grayson shrugged. The kid was struggling, alright. Dirk could tell by the way Molly interacted with him. Constantly at his side, urging him to pet her in an effort to distract him from whatever tormented him. The same way she did with Dirk. Though, in his case, it seemed that didn't happen as often as it used to.

Dirk thought back to that first day Grayson showed up here. His defiant, mad-at-the-world attitude. Yet the two of them had found their way past that to build a friendship. And, until yesterday, Dirk had thought he was making a difference in the kid's life. But the venom Grayson had spewed at Tessa suggested otherwise.

When the boy remained silent, Dirk grabbed the next

cabinet and set to work. And so things continued until it was time for lunch.

Dirk descended the ladder. "I don't know about you, but I'm ready for some lunch. And I've got a pimento cheese sandwich in the cooler that's calling my name." He dragged the back of his hand over his brow. "Care to join me? I brought two."

Grayson shook his head as they continued onto the porch. "I'm not hungry."

Not hungry? The kid was always hungry. Perhaps he'd already tapped into his own lunch.

"Can I play with Molly instead?"

"Yes." He removed Molly's vest. "If you change your mind, just let me know."

After retrieving one of the sandwiches, along with a bag of chips and another of grapes from his cooler, Dirk settled into the camp chair he kept on the porch as Grayson and Molly played ball on the side of the cabin. Thankfully, today's humidity was tolerable. Throw in a light breeze and it was downright pleasant. Well, the weather, anyway.

He checked his phone, hoping he might find a text from Tessa. Nothing. She must be working on that shiplap. Her plan had been to start priming today. Though, after yesterday's drama, she might not feel up to it. The situation with Grayson had left her sad, angry, frustrated and who knew what else. So he did the only thing he knew to do. Bowed his head and pleaded with God to bring healing to Tessa's family.

With his lunch gone, he stood and returned the empty containers to the cooler, then checked the side of the house for Grayson and Molly. When they weren't there, he checked the other side, but came up empty-handed once again.

"Grayson?" He continued around to the back of the house. And there on the stoop he found Grayson hugging his knees to his chest while Molly whined and repeatedly licked him, desperate to do her job and distract him.

The sight broke Dirk's heart.

Moving alongside the boy, he knelt. "Grayson?" He kept his voice gentle, not wanting to startle him. "Talk to me, buddy. What's going on?"

The boy sobbed, his body jerking. "My dad is dead." He hiccupped. "Because of my mom."

Dirk felt as though he'd been hit upside the head with a two-by-four. For a moment, he just sat there, trying to figure out how or why Grayson could think such a thing. "No." Dirk shook his head. "Grayson, that's not true. Why would you even think that?"

"Because my Gigi said so."

Just when Dirk thought he couldn't be any more shocked than he already was. "Gigi is your grandmother?" Tessa's mother-in-law. The one Grayson spoke with yesterday.

Grayson nodded.

"What did she say exactly?"

The boy unfurled his legs and Molly used that as an opportunity to lay her head in Grayson's lap. "That my dad was dead because of my mom. I heard her tell Pops." Grayson wrapped his arms around the dog.

Meanwhile, Dirk felt as though his head might explode. "Is that your grandfather?"

The kid lifted his head to nod, his cheeks ruddy and tear stained.

"Did Gigi know you could hear her?"

The tormented boy shook his head. "They were in their bedroom with the door closed." He sniffed. "I was going to ask them something, but then I heard her crying." He began sobbing again.

"How long ago was this?"

The boy shrugged, holding tightly to Molly.

"Was it recently?"

Grayson shook his head. "Before we came here last summer."

Last summer? That was a long time for a little boy to carry such a huge burden. That would explain his change in behavior, though. Why he'd started acting out. But why would Grayson's grandmother blame Tessa for her husband's death?

He remembered Tessa saying her husband refused to get help. Was there more she could've done? Or was what Grayson overheard simply a grief-stricken mother trying to make sense of the death of her child?

Dirk suspected the latter. Sadly, Grayson's grandmother had caused an already hurting family even more pain.

A breeze rustled through the trees overhead, and Dirk pulled in a breath. *God, I could use a whole lot of help here. Please.*

"Grayson, you've known your mom your whole life. Do you believe she would've hurt your dad?"

The kid sniffed as he thought. "I heard them fighting. Then my dad left." His voice sounded strangled. "When I woke up, he was dead."

Oh, how Dirk wished he could explain to Grayson that his father hadn't been in his right mind. That the TBI had changed him from a loving father to someone his son struggled to recognize. But that wasn't Dirk's story to tell.

"Unfortunately, married people fight sometimes." Like he and Lindsey had the night of the crash. If Dirk could have one do-over, that would be it. "Grayson, look at me."

It took a moment, but he finally did.

"You need to tell your mom what you just told me—what your Gigi said—and then give your mom an opportunity to tell her side of the story."

Panic had his eyes widening. "But she'll be mad at me."

"Grayson, I don't usually make promises. But I promise your mom will *not* be mad at you."

The kid dug his fingers into Molly's fur as he contemplated. Then he looked up at Dirk. "Would you come with me?"

Oh, boy. What had he gotten himself into? Served him right for bringing up Grayson's behavior yesterday. Now he could only pray that Tessa wouldn't be upset with him for getting involved.

"Yes, I will go with you."

# Chapter Nine

Tessa stood in Aunt Dee's living room, admiring the freshly primed shiplap. The effort, along with a TobyMac marathon via her earbuds, had provided a much-needed diversion from yesterday's drama.

Grayson thought she hated him. That she'd hated Nick.

Tears pricked her eyes once again. Had the claim simply been one of a hurting little boy lashing out? Or did he truly believe it?

Whatever the case, it had turned what was supposed to be a day of fun upside down. Dirk had even had to drive them back while she tried to console a sobbing Bryce.

After returning from the swimming hole, Grayson had gone straight to his bed and stayed there the rest of the night.

Meanwhile, Bryce struggled to process his brother's claims. He wasn't the only one. And she had no idea where to go from here.

When would the fallout from Nick's death come to an end? Or would it go on forever, tormenting Grayson? Tormenting her.

Those and countless other questions had her sobbing into her pillow until the wee hours of this morning. So when Dee took Grayson to the cabin after breakfast, Tessa gave in to Bryce's pleas to watch a movie in the family room, then set to work on the shiplap. And as lunchtime approached, she had something to show for her efforts. All she had left to do now was paint the shiplap. Then they could start putting the space back together.

Dirk had offered to reattach all of the trim. But before he could do that, they'd need to remove the worn carpet. Dee had decided to expose the original wood flooring and go with area rugs instead. Something that pleased Tessa very much.

Hearing Aunt Dee's truck outside, Tessa grabbed the paint tray holding a brush and a small roller and took them to the utility sink in the laundry room to clean them. She turned on the water as Dee entered.

"Hey, sugar." Dee gave her a one-arm squeeze. "How you doin'?"

Tessa could only shrug. If she opened her mouth she was apt to start crying again.

"Where's Bryce?" her aunt asked.

Tessa cleared her throat. "In the family room, watching TV." When his movie ended, she'd allowed him to watch a show.

"I need to run into Hope Crossing to Plowmans. Thought he and I could grab some lunch. Course some of their *kolaches* are apt to follow us home, too." With a loving touch, her aunt brushed Tessa's hair away from her face. "You need anything?"

Besides putting her world back to rights? If only it was that simple.

Shaking her head, Tessa focused on the paint tray. And by the time she finished cleaning everything, her aunt and Bryce had gone. But not before Bryce gave her an extra big hug. He looked up at her with those sweet brown eyes and said, "It'll be okay, Mama."

Oh, to have his faith.

Her gaze drifted to the wood-plank ceiling as she moved

into the kitchen. "God, I know You're there. But I could really use You right here, right now." She wound her arms around her torso. Life had been an uphill battle these last few years. And she wasn't sure how much more she could take. "God, please, show me how to help Grayson."

She looked down at Nash, who'd been trailing her, and gave him a rub before opening the refrigerator. Staring at the contents, she knew she should eat something, but nothing sounded appealing. She'd managed a piece of toast for breakfast, along with multiple cups of coffee. Running on so little sleep, she needed a boost.

Suddenly the dog woofed and started toward the hall.

Startled, she tossed the door closed and followed him. "What is it, boy?"

As she entered the hall, she saw Grayson crossing the threshold at the other end, Molly on his heels, much to Nash's delight. Dirk brought up the rear and, based on their grim expressions, she wasn't going to like what he had to say.

Had Grayson done something? Was Dirk not willing to work with him anymore?

"Wh-what's going on?" Wrapping her arms around her waist, she remained where she was.

"Grayson has some things he'd like to tell you." Dirk closed the door before putting a hand on her son's shoulder. "Is there someplace we could all sit down?"

All? That meant Dirk was staying. And she was surprised at the measure of comfort that gave her.

"Um, we can go in the family room." Turning, she started that way. "Aunt Dee and Bryce just left."

"I know," said Dirk. "I spoke with her."

Tessa's steps slowed as he and Grayson neared, her gaze lifting to Dirk's.

His gray-blue eyes were filled with compassion. "I thought it would be best if we were alone."

The statement had her wondering if she should be more nervous or relieved. But she was thankful he was here.

She led the way into the family room off of the kitchen. The second-most-used space in the house boasted the same paneling she'd removed from the living room, along with tan ceramic-tile flooring topped with a large rust and brown latch-hook rug her grandmother had made back in the 1970s.

Easing onto one end of the leather sofa, she motioned for Grayson to sit beside her.

He paused, one hand on Molly while he looked at Dirk as though silently asking if he had to. Then she noticed his tear-streaked cheeks.

While her son was seemingly still debating the move, Dirk settled himself on the end opposite her. "It's okay, Grayson."

Finally, he perched on the edge of the center cushion. Molly stood beside him while Nash dropped alongside Tessa.

Eyeing her over her son's head, Dirk said, "Grayson shared something with me a little while ago that I think will shed some light on his actions yesterday."

She looked from Dirk to her son. While she was glad Grayson felt comfortable enough to share things with Dirk, she was disappointed he hadn't felt comfortable coming to her.

"When me and Bryce were at Gigi and Pops's last year." He stroked Molly's head, his gaze fixed on the dog. "Before we came to the ranch last summer. I heard Gigi crying in her room. And she told Pops my dad was dead because of you."

While Tessa had willed herself to listen calmly, she couldn't help her sharp intake of breath. "Because of…me?" Her gaze darted to Dirk, then back to her son.

A tear fell onto Grayson's cheek as he hugged Molly. "I

heard you and Dad fighting that night." He sniffed. "He left. And never came back."

The urge to wrap her arms around her little boy and make all the pain go away nearly overwhelmed her. But she was afraid he'd pull away from her once again.

"Oh, Gray, your dad was different when he came back from his last tour of duty."

"Cuz the explosion gave him a brain inj'ry."

"Yes. He tried really hard to pretend everything was okay. But his mind didn't function the way it used to. That frustrated him and made him angry." Not at all like the laid-back Nick she'd always known. That Nick never would've put his fist through a wall. Or snapped at his children for no apparent reason.

"How come the doctors didn't help him?"

"They tried. But your daddy didn't want their help. He thought he could fix himself. But he couldn't. And that upset him even more. No matter how much I begged him to get help, he still refused. That's what we were fighting about when he left." A tear trailed down her cheek, but she dashed it away.

"How come Gigi said it was your fault he died?"

She sucked in a breath. "I don't know. But what I do know is that she was very sad." To the point that she'd gone into a deep depression for a time. Now that Tessa thought about it, it was about the time she and the boys had come to the ranch last year that Dan had gotten Gina into grief counseling. "Emotions can be very powerful, making us do things and act in ways we might not otherwise." Like impacting Grayson's behavior.

"Grayson?"

He finally looked at her as Molly laid her head in his lap.

"Have you ever shared what happened with your counselor?"

His gaze fell away as he shook his head.

"Oh, Grayson." She wrapped him in her arms, praying he wouldn't pull away. "Your daddy's death impacted all of us. We're all struggling with emotions we've never had before. That's why it's important we talk about them. Otherwise, they build up inside of us like bubbles in a soda can, until something pops our top and then they spew all over and make a mess."

"Like I did yesterday."

She set him away from her then. "Exactly like that." Smoothing that beautiful auburn hair away from his face, she smiled. "I love you, Grayson. So much. I wish you had told me what Gigi said instead of keeping it to yourself. That must've left you feeling very confused and conflicted."

He nodded.

"I'm your mom. I know you better than anyone, and you can tell me anything. Good or bad. Even stuff you think I might not like. But, please, do it in a respectful manner. When you lash out, it hurts my heart, and then I'm apt to respond in a way you might not like. And that doesn't do any of us any good."

His bottom lip trembled. "I'm sorry, Mama."

Pulling him to her once again, she breathed in sweat mingled with that little boy scent. "I'm sorry, too." She lifted her gaze to find Dirk watching them. What an incredible man he was. She had no doubt God had brought him into their lives for a reason. His willingness to take on a hurting little boy may very well bring the healing they so desperately need.

"Thank you." She mouthed the words.

His smile had her recalling the teaching position Aunt Dee had mentioned yesterday. Perhaps Tessa should consider applying after all. That is, if her sons concurred.

* * *

Dirk's admiration for Tessa had catapulted to another level Monday afternoon. Sitting in Ms. D'Lynn's family room as Grayson painfully unpacked the burden he'd carried for the past year was no easy task. Yet Tessa had listened patiently before responding with the kind of unconditional love every child deserved. And it was now reflected in her son's attitude.

Since Tuesday morning, Dirk felt as though he was working with a different child. Grayson smiled more, even joked with Dirk. Last night at Ms. D'Lynn's, he'd invited his brother to play in the hillbilly hot tub while Dirk and Tessa put the living room trim back in place.

Dirk thanked God the boy had trusted him enough to open up. And as a result, begun the process of healing their family.

Now, with the cabin's new Sheetrock walls in the bathroom and one side of the kitchen finally painted, Dirk found himself monitoring the drive for any sign of Tessa as he cleaned the brushes with the hose Wednesday afternoon. While Bryce got to spend the day at his new friend Owen's house, Tessa had gone to Houston to speak face-to-face with her in-laws. And though Dirk hadn't heard from her, she'd been in his prayers all day.

Tessa was a special woman, alright. The kind who could make him change his mind about falling in love again. Something he'd vowed he'd never do.

Turning off the water, he promptly dismissed the notion. She was only here for the summer, so he'd do well to keep his heart in check.

"Mr. Dirk?" Grayson sat on the porch step, absently petting Molly while he watched Dirk.

Shaking the excess water from the brushes, he said, "What's up?"

The kid peered up at him with those dark eyes. "How come you're not married?"

Whoa. Nothing like a curveball. Had the kid been reading his mind?

"I used to be." He cringed, realizing the can of worms he'd likely opened.

The kid stared at him, seemingly perplexed. "What happened?"

With a sigh, Dirk settled on the other side of Molly and wiped the sweat from his brow. "My wife and little girl died in a car accident. The same one that took part of my leg." He gestured, finding it strange how he'd learned to talk about the event so matter-of-factly.

Grayson's eyes went wide, his mouth falling open. "When?"

"Five years ago." Dirk shifted his prosthetic to a more comfortable position. "Emory—my daughter—was only four." He watched Grayson process the information.

"She'd be nine like me." The boy hung his head. "Well, if she hadn't died."

"Yes, she would."

A cow bellowed from the pasture behind the cabin, likely calling her calf.

Turning his dark gaze on Dirk again, Grayson said, "You must miss them."

"I do. Just like you miss your dad."

The sound of tires on gravel had them looking toward the road as Tessa's SUV came into view. Obviously Grayson had been anticipating her arrival every bit as much as Dirk, since they both stood while she parked.

Grayson jogged toward her as she stepped out of the vehicle, looking far more at ease than she had when she left this morning. And it did Dirk's heart good when Grayson wrapped his arms around her middle and hugged her. Something Dirk was certain Tessa appreciated, too.

*Thank You, God.*

"Well—" Dirk approached them "—how did it go?"

Dressed in a denim skirt and a sleeveless brown blouse, Tessa took a deep breath and smiled. "It went very well. I think it was good for us to get everything out in the open." She set an arm around Grayson's shoulders. "Gigi was very sad and ashamed when I told her what you'd overheard. She admitted she'd been in a bad way the night you heard her say those things. And it was right after that Pops saw to it she got the help *she* needed."

"But why did she blame you?" Grayson peered up at his mother.

Shaking her head, she said, "Because we don't like it when we can't make sense of things. And that often has us looking for something or someone to blame. Since I was the person closest to your dad—" she shrugged "—she blamed me."

The kid's face contorted. "I wish I hadn't heard her say that stuff."

She smoothed a hand over his sweaty hair. "We all do, Gray. But I'm glad you finally brought it to my attention so we could learn the truth and free you from that burden." She dropped a kiss atop his head before releasing him. "Oh, and Gigi and Pops are coming for July Fourth with a surprise."

Grayson's eyes lit up. "What kind of surprise?"

"They didn't tell me, so it'll be a surprise to all of us." She turned her attention to Dirk then. "Which reminds me, you and your family are invited to Aunt Dee's annual Fourth of July shindig, featuring some of the best barbecue in Texas, all kinds of fun and the best fireworks show in the county."

"Sounds like fun."

"It's *so* fun," Grayson concurred. "We have a waterslide and there's music and so much food." Licking his chops, he rubbed his belly.

Dirk couldn't help laughing. He'd never seen Grayson so animated. "Sounds like quite the event." One he was suddenly looking forward to attending.

"You have no idea," said Tessa. "Which is why I won't be starting on the dining room until it's over."

"Mom—" Grayson looked up at her "—did you apply for that job?"

Her suddenly nervous gaze darted to Dirk before returning to her son.

"What job?" Dirk couldn't help asking.

"Oops." Grayson covered his mouth with his hand. "I wasn't s'posed to say anything."

Smiling, Tessa shook her head as she turned her attention to Dirk. "They're looking for a new second-grade teacher at the elementary school in Hope Crossing. After talking with the boys, we've decided I should apply." Turning her attention to Grayson, she added, "However, I have been gone all day, so, no, I've not had time to do it yet. But I will."

"Tomorrow?"

Shaking her head, she ruffled the boy's hair. "Tomorrow."

"If she gets it, we get to live at the ranch." The kid bounced on the balls of his sneakers.

It did Dirk's heart good to see Grayson so happy for a change.

Yet as he recalled the conversation he'd had with Tessa the night they took the boys fishing, Dirk shifted his attention to her. "And you said you weren't courageous."

She lifted a shoulder, those pretty hazel eyes sparkling. "I guess you've had a positive influence on me."

"Glad I could help." Yet looking at her now, he was suddenly aware of the influence she was starting to have on him, too. If she was to stay at Legacy Ranch, he might not be able to ignore it any longer.

# Chapter Ten

"Hold this, please." With the afternoon sun filtering through the leaves in Aunt Dee's backyard and the temperature in the low nineties, Tessa handed one end of the banner bearing red, white and blue pennant flags to Dirk.

"I still can't get over this." Beneath the canopy of oak trees draped with white lights, Dirk took in Aunt Dee's backyard, where pots of red, white and purple petunias adorned with miniature American flags graced round tables covered with either red or blue plastic tablecloths. "I've never known anyone who went all out like this for Independence Day."

"Welcome to the Fourth of July at Legacy Ranch." Tessa couldn't help smiling. This was Aunt Dee's favorite event of the year. Even more so than Christmas. "It's my aunt's way of letting her family, friends and employees know how much she loves and appreciates them."

Around these parts, Legacy Ranch's July Fourth celebration was the event of the season. And with her sisters also here to enjoy the festivities, Tessa had resolved to relax and enjoy herself.

So, in the two weeks since applying for the teaching position via the school district's website, she'd kept busy prepping the house and yard for today's event. While she'd decided to hold off on removing the paneling in the dining room until after today, the living room had to be put to rights. It now boasted a new area rug over the freshly uncovered wood floors. And despite the same old furnishings—which Aunt Dee was already talking about replacing—the space looked fresh and inviting.

Then, since the rest of the house had pretty much been ignored while Tessa put all her efforts into her quest for ship-lap, she given everything a good cleaning. Anything to prevent her from parking on the notion of moving to the ranch. She did not want to get her hopes up.

Her sons, on the other hand, refused to be deterred, despite her constant warnings. Bryce had even added his plea to his nightly prayers. She envied his childlike faith. Sadly, she'd spent more time dwelling on unanswered prayers than trusting God with her desires.

*What about Nick's parents?* her conscience prodded. She'd feared the worst when she'd visited Dan and Gina. Yet God had brought some much-needed healing out of that difficult situation.

*Thank You, God.*

"My parents are going to be sorry they had to miss it." Despite the invitation, Dirk's folks had already made plans.

"There's always next year." Taking the other end of the banner from him, she realized what she'd said. As her cheeks heated, she quickly saw to her task, hoping he hadn't noticed.

"Mom!" Wearing his swim trunks and a sun shirt, Grayson hollered from the far side of the house while Molly kept a close eye on him. "Somebody's here." He motioned for her to follow him. "You gotta come see this."

Tessa glanced at her watch. It wasn't even three. A little early for guests. Unless it was her in-laws. But Grayson would've said something, wouldn't he?

She glanced at Dirk. "Let's go see what all the fuss is about."

Weaving her way through tables, she followed the path her son had taken before coming to an abrupt halt when she spotted a motor home in the drive. And it was towing her in-laws' SUV.

Suddenly, the passenger door opened, and Gina slid out of her seat. "Surprise!" Sporting tortoiseshell Jackie O sunglasses and a short-sleeved stars and stripes tunic over navy shorts, she struck a pose reminiscent of a television game show model.

"Whoa!" Grayson stared at the massive vehicle. "Is that yours?"

Bryce appeared from out of nowhere, rushing his grandmother as Dan rounded the front of the motor home.

"We told you we had a surprise." Dan intercepted the kid, twirling him around before setting his feet back on the gravel.

"I know—" Tessa started toward them "—but I never expected anything like this."

"We decided we needed to shake things up a bit." Gina slipped her arm through her husband's. "You know, a change of scenery."

Tessa eyed the motor coach. "That will most certainly do it."

"Can I go inside?" The genuine excitement in Grayson's eyes warmed Tessa's heart.

"Me, too." Bryce peered up at his grandfather.

"Oh. My. Word." Aunt Dee's disbelieving voice came from the front porch before she hurried down the steps wearing a star-spangled shirt over denim shorts. "What have y'all gone and done?"

Gina greeted her with a hug. "We are embarking on an adventure."

"I'll say." Noticing Dirk a few feet away, hands in the pockets of his navy shorts, Molly at his side, Dee waved him over. "Gina, I'd like you to meet Dirk Matthews. He's been workin' on some projects around the ranch for me."

"It's nice to meet you, Dir—" Gina's eyes widened. "Wait, you're Dirk?" She held up a hand. "Excuse me a moment." Turning, she hollered for her husband.

When he looked her way, she waved him over.

Leaving the boys to explore the RV, Dan hurried their way. "Whatcha need?"

Taking hold of his elbow, she gestured toward Dirk with her free hand. "*This* is Dirk." Gina was almost breathless as she made the announcement.

Tessa had told them how Dirk had been instrumental in getting Grayson to reveal what he'd been holding inside for far too long. Something she would be eternally grateful for. Because of Dirk, she had her son back. And the knowledge of that was doing strange things to her heart.

Dan's smile matched his wife's as the two men shook hands. "Good to meet you, Dirk. Dan Wagner." Letting go, his gaze fell to the dog. "And this must be Molly." Addressing Dirk once again, he added, "We've heard a lot about both of you."

"Oh?" Dirk looked confused, and Tessa suddenly felt sorry for him. She probably should've given him a heads-up.

"Grayson has told us how much he enjoys working with you and Molly," said Gina.

Dirk finally smiled. "He's a good worker."

Hands in the pockets of his golf shorts, Dan rocked back on the heels of his deck shoes. "We can't thank you enough for all you've done for him. For all of us, really."

In that moment, Tessa felt as though all was right in her world. Something she hadn't felt in a very long time.

"Why don't y'all come on in and grab yourselves some lemonade," said Dee.

"That sounds lovely." Gina followed her. "Is there anything I can do to help you get ready?"

"Oh, I'm sure there is." Dee chuckled.

"I'd like to see that RV." Tessa grinned at her father-in-law.

"You got it. Dirk, why don't you come, too."

As soon as they stepped inside, the boys were begging to sleep over. And by the time the tour was complete, guests were arriving, so Tessa and her sisters took turns greeting folks and directing them around back.

In no time, young and old alike were enjoying the inflatable waterslide Dee had rented, while country music spilled from Bluetooth speakers scattered around the yard. A couple of toddlers splashed about in the hillbilly hot tub as their parents took pictures, while a group of older men gathered around the horseshoe pit farther away. Other folks mingled about, sipping cold beverages while noshing on chips and salsa, bacon-wrapped stuffed jalapenos and fruit.

The boys went up and down the waterslide with Bryce's new friend Owen, while Dan and Dirk watched them, chatting up a storm. Seemed all her worries about them meeting had been for naught. But then, Dirk was a likeable guy. Perhaps a little too likeable.

Suddenly, he started her way. And that smile had her heart beating out a staccato.

"Everything okay?" he asked as he stopped beside her.

"Mmm-hmm." Oh, she sounded way too chipper. Time to tone things down. "I'm just watching everyone have fun."

"I forgot to mention, you look beautiful today." Those incredible gray-blue eyes stayed fixed on hers. "Red is definitely your color."

Smoothing a hand over her sundress, she couldn't recall the last time she'd received a compliment on her appearance.

She dipped her head, slightly. "Thank you."

"Tessa?" Meredith waved from the back door. "We need you."

Tessa nodded before returning her attention to Dirk, uncertain as to whether she was annoyed or relieved. "It's time to bring the food out. Would you mind keeping an eye on the boys for me?"

"Not at all. I'll save you a seat."

Tessa and her sisters had been to so many of Legacy Ranch's July Fourth events that they knew just where to put everything. The smoked brisket, chicken and sausage, along with the pinto beans and macaroni and cheese were served in large restaurant-style chafing pans on one table alongside sliced bread, sliced pickles and onions and, of course, jalapenos. Meanwhile large bowls of coleslaw, potato salad and fruit salad were nestled in ice-filled inflatable buffet coolers on a separate table.

Once the food was in place, Aunt Dee made a brief speech welcoming everyone before blessing the food. Then it was time to dig in.

Tessa and her sisters kept watch, bringing more food from the kitchen as needed, until the line had dwindled. Then they fixed their own plates, and Tessa joined Gina, Dan, Dirk and her boys.

"Everything was delicious." Dan pushed his plate away and patted his belly as Tessa was digging into her mac and cheese.

"I hope you left room for dessert." She nabbed a small forkful. "There's peach cobbler, cookies and brownies."

"In that case—" he pushed his chair back "—anyone care to join me?"

"Me!" her boys said simultaneously.

Beside her, Dirk set his napkin atop his plate. "I guess I'll go, too." Looking at Gina and Tessa, he said, "Can I bring you ladies anything?"

"Peach cobbler would be lovely," said Gina. "Thank you, Dirk."

"My pleasure. Tessa?"

"I'm good for now." She motioned to the dog lying between them. "Molly can stay with me, if you'd like."

With a nod he was on his way.

And Tessa couldn't help noticing Gina watching him retreat. After a moment, she turned her attention to Tessa, her expression suddenly serious. "Tessa, there's something I feel like I need to say."

With a fork full of mac and cheese in her right hand, Tessa reached for Molly with her left, her heart dropping. Had today brought back memories of coming to this same event with Nick? Was Gina upset? What if watching Dirk interact with her grandsons had reopened the wounds of her son's death?

"You are a beautiful young woman," Gina began. "And you deserve to find love again."

Tessa nearly choked. "I'm sorry, what?"

"You heard me." Her mother-in-law gave an emphatic nod.

"Gina, if this is about Dirk, he and I are just friends."

The other woman looked across the patio to where Dirk stood holding a bowl of cobbler as he chatted with Bryce. "Hmph. What a shame." She turned back to Tessa. "He's quite the looker."

Tessa stifled a chuckle. "*Gina*, what has gotten into you?"

"I don't know." The woman guffawed. "But isn't it wonderful?"

Tessa couldn't help laughing. Yes, it was wonderful. And terrifying at the same time.

Dirk pulled up to Ms. D'Lynn's two days later, trying to remember the last time he'd enjoyed himself as much as he had at her July Fourth event. Not that he got out much. Still, for the first time since the accident, he'd felt almost normal. Interacting with so many people—some he was familiar with, many he was not—had been a pleasure instead of a chore. He might've even gained a client or two.

And to his surprise, spending time with Dan and Gina had been pleasurable, as opposed to the drudgery he'd anticipated. Dan and Gina were great people. Nothing at all like he'd envisioned them to be. Making him even more thankful he'd been able to play a tiny role in their family's healing.

Of course, the best part of the day had been sharing it with Tessa and her boys. Sitting beside her as they watched fireworks that evening, the scent of her shampoo beckoning him to inch ever closer, had his heart booming right along with those rockets.

Now, Molly whined beside him, and he caught a glimpse of his goofy smile in the rearview mirror. Yeah, he needed to shut down that train of thought immediately. He couldn't afford the distraction when he was about to present his proposal for the bunkhouse to Ms. D'Lynn and her nieces.

Since Meredith, Audrey and Kendall were staying through the weekend, it made sense for them to meet so they could go over things in person. Even if he'd rather be removing the paneling in Ms. D'Lynn's dining room with Tessa.

He mentally chided himself. So he enjoyed her company.

It was only because she understood him in a way few people could.

*Keep telling yourself that, buddy.*

Frowning, he snagged his computer bag from the floorboard and opened the door. The humid afternoon air wasted no time wrapping around him as he waited for Molly to exit. What he wouldn't give for a dip in the swimming hole with Tessa and the boys.

The front door opened as they started up the walk, and a smiling Grayson stepped onto the porch in his bare feet.

Molly bounded up the steps.

Meanwhile, Dirk still marveled at the kid's transformation. All glory to God, on that one. Dirk just counted himself blessed that God had been able to use him in some small way to help bring it about.

"What, were you watching for me?"

The kid nodded, petting Molly. "It's crazy in there."

Dirk could hear the women's chatter coming from the kitchen. "Why do you say that?"

"'Cause my mom and her sisters are weird."

"Dirk." A winded Tessa appeared behind her son.

"What's got you all out of breath?"

"Oh, we were just revisiting childhood memories. Come on in."

Continuing into the center hall, Dirk caught himself inhaling her sweet scent, as though he needed it to survive. "Sounds rather lively back there." He nodded toward the kitchen.

"We spent the morning at the cabin, unpacking all the stuff we bought yesterday." Tessa closed the door as Nash trotted toward them. "Everything from a coffee maker, dishes and silverware to pillows and bedding for a bed we don't even have yet."

He'd heard one of the sisters suggest a shopping trip during the party. He could only imagine what a rousing adventure it must've been with the four of them and their aunt. But—

"What did you do with Grayson and Bryce?"

"She made us go, too." Still petting Molly, Grayson frowned. "It was *so* boring."

Looping an arm around his neck, his mother said, "Hey, you got Chick-fil-A and ice cream, so stop complaining." Returning her attention to Dirk, she added, "Dee didn't want to be away from the ranch for too long, so we only went to Brenham."

"Well, if I'd've known you were going, the boys could've hung out with me."

Grayson looked at his mother. "See. I told you he'd watch us."

Pink tinged her cheeks as she worried her bottom lip. "I didn't know if you were working, so I didn't want to bother you."

"I get it. But next time, feel free to bother me."

"Oh, you're here." Meredith—Tessa's older sister—strolled through the hall from the kitchen. "We were wondering where you were."

"Sorry, I got distracted." Dirk couldn't help noticing the way her gaze kept darting between him and Tessa.

"Why don't you set up in the dining room while I let everyone know you're here."

Dirk leaned toward Tessa as Meredith returned to the kitchen. "I don't think she likes me."

"Don't be offended." Tessa motioned for him to follow her. "That's just Meredith."

Grayson went first. "Can Molly hang out in the family room with me?"

"Where's your brother?" Dirk asked as he followed them through the welcoming living room.

"Watching *Hero Squad.*"

"That's one of my favorite movies." Now in the dining room, Dirk set his backpack on a chair.

"Mine, too." Grayson's dark eyes lit up. "And there's a new one coming out. *Hero Squad: Battle for Tomorrow.*"

"I heard. Perhaps we could all go see it together."

The kid grabbed hold of his mother's arm. "Can we, Mom?"

"I'm sure we can work something out." She glanced up at Dirk. "Can I get you something to drink?"

"Water would be great, thank you." He unpacked his laptop and turned it on as the other women joined them.

"Dirk, you did a spectacular job on the cabin." Kendall took a seat across the table.

"Thank you. I'm glad you approve. Though, a lot of thanks goes to my helper here." He patted Grayson on the back.

"That's pretty cool, Gray. You got to be a part of the cabin's transformation."

"Hello, Dirk." Ms. D'Lynn continued toward the far end of the table with a glass of iced tea as Bryce whisked into the space.

"Ms. D'Lynn." Dirk nodded, holding up a palm for a high five from Bryce. "How's it going, Bryce?"

"Good." He hugged Molly.

"Yeah, Grayson." Their aunt settled into her seat as Meredith joined them. "You'll always have a connection with the cabin that nobody else will."

The boy turned thoughtful. "I guess it is kinda cool." He shrugged.

"Boys," Tessa called from the kitchen. "Come watch your movie."

"Bye, Dirk." Bryce raced out of the room.

"Bye, Dirk." And Grayson was on his heels.

"So are you really thinking about moving to the ranch?" Audrey eyed Tessa as they walked in together a few seconds later.

Holding two waters, Tessa said, "I've applied for a teaching position in Hope Crossing. That's it. There are no guarantees that it will pan out." She set one glass beside him.

"Thank you."

"But you would move out here if you got it." Audrey took the seat beside Kendall.

Tessa sucked in a breath, a clue she was frustrated. Probably because she didn't want the boys getting their hopes up. Perhaps she should've kept the info from Dirk, too.

Settling into the chair next to him, she said, "Yes, that would be the logical thing to do."

"I know some great real estate agents in your neighborhood," Audrey added. "That area is very desirable. It wouldn't be a surprise if you got an offer within days."

Meredith observed things from the other end of the table. "How do the boys feel about changing schools?"

"Girls!" Ms. D'Lynn was either trying to rescue Tessa or get all of them back on task.

Dirk couldn't help admiring the way she managed to keep things in order. Whether it was scrappy ranch hands, the ranch itself or her family.

Once he'd pulled the design up on his computer, Dirk turned it so the women could see the 3D rendering on the screen as he walked them through it.

"You're adding a second floor?" Audrey pointed.

"That's actually a loft where the kids—or adults—can sleep. That way you'll still have a small sitting area down here—" he pointed "—with a pullout sleeper for additional sleeping."

"What a great idea." Ms. D'Lynn smiled.

"Wish I could take credit for it, but that was Tessa's suggestion." He looked her way, unable to hold back his smile.

"I just asked myself what I would appreciate as a mom."

For the better part of the next hour, the sisters asked questions and discussed materials and design. Other than a few minor tweaks, they seemed pleased.

"I printed out copies of the floor plan for each of you." Digging through his bag, he was unable to locate them. "I'll be right back. I think I left them in my truck."

He hurried outside and spotted the folder as soon as he opened the door. Grabbing them, he noticed Meredith coming toward him.

"Before we go back in." She glanced over her shoulder as if making sure no one was coming. "My sisters and I can't help noticing how taken with you our nephews are. Seems every time they open their mouths your name comes out."

"They're good kids. I enjoy their company."

"We appreciate what you've done for Grayson. Getting him to open up and reveal what's been weighing on him." Smiling, she shook her head. "It does all of our hearts good to see him happy again."

Dirk was starting to feel uneasy. As if a simple thank-you wasn't all Tessa's older sister had on her mind.

"Audrey, Kendall and I are a little concerned, though," she continued.

"About what?"

"Tessa and her boys have been through a lot these last few years. Not only with Nick's injury and subsequent death, but our father passed early this year. So, as you can imagine, my sisters and I are rather protective of them."

Sweat trailed down his cheek as he narrowed his gaze. "Are you suggesting I pose some sort of threat to Tessa and her boys?"

Meredith squared her shoulders. "I don't know you well enough to conclude that, Dirk. Although, my aunt thinks very highly of you. I just wanted you to be aware that we Hunts are a protective lot. When one hurts, we all hurt. And my sister has endured enough pain."

"I understand. And I appreciate your concern. However, I think you're misconstruing things. Tessa and I are just friends. Having lost our spouses, we're able to understand each other in ways most people can't." Yet even as he said the words he wondered who he was trying to convince more. Meredith or himself.

# Chapter Eleven

"**S**he did what?" Tessa burst into Kendall's room Sunday morning to stare at her and Audrey.

"Tessa?" Standing beside the unmade full-size bed, where Kendall sat putting on her makeup, Audrey looked the same way she had when Aunt Dee caught her sneaking into the house after midnight when she was fifteen. "I-I thought you were downstairs."

"Well, you thought wrong." She glared at her sisters. "What do you mean Meredith warned Dirk? Warned him about what?"

Her sisters shared a look.

Fists balling at her sides, Tessa was tempted to go directly to her older sister, but she was downstairs—and so were the boys.

"She was only trying to protect you," Kendall offered.

"Protect me from what?"

"From having your heart broken again."

Tessa whirled to find Meredith standing in the doorway, her brown hair slicked back into its usual tight bun. "What?" She moved toward her. "Dirk and I are friends. Why can't you seem to understand that?"

"Oh, please." Already dressed for church in black slacks, a cream blouse and a pair of black low-heeled sandals—

a minor variation of her standard black-and-white color scheme—Meredith strolled into the room with her holier-than-thou attitude. "You're as smitten with him as the boys are. And, dare I say, the feeling is mutual."

No wonder Dirk had hightailed it out of here after giving them the copies of his design.

Crossing her arms, Tessa stepped closer, shaking her head. "You just can't stand to see us happy for a change, can you? You think that, because you're miserable, everyone else should be, too. I mean, God forbid we have any kind of joy in our lives."

"That's *enough*, girls!"

Turning, they spotted Aunt Dee in the doorway, hands on her hips, looking as though she was ready to take down an angry bull.

And making Tessa feel like she was fourteen again.

Shaking her head, their aunt continued into the room, wearing a short-sleeve floral blouse over dark wash jeans and her cream-colored Sunday cowboy boots. "What are you doin', actin' like a couple of bullheaded teenagers?"

Suddenly realizing everyone was there except Grayson and Bryce, Tessa glanced at her aunt. "Where are the boys?"

"I told them to take Nash outside."

"Okay, good." She did not want the boys to know what her sister had done. Arms crossed, she glared at Meredith, who stood in front of the window adorned with lace curtains. "Are you going to tell her or am I?"

"She's angry because I had a little talk with Dirk yesterday."

Aunt Dee's gaze narrowed. "About what?"

Meredith lifted her chin in a manner Tessa couldn't decide was arrogant or defiant. "I wanted to make sure he understood that we are protective of each other. Tessa and the boys have suffered enough loss."

"And Dirk hasn't?" Tessa couldn't help herself. "Or have you forgotten he lost his wife and daughter?"

"I have not. But the boys can't seem to stop talking about him."

"That's because he's had a positive influence on their lives. He's done more for my family these last six weeks than a year of counseling. Especially Grayson. Because of Dirk, I actually have a relationship with my son again."

Looking as though she'd been slapped, Meredith lowered her gaze. "I only wanted to protect you. The way Dad would have."

"Where is everybody?" Bryce's voice filtered up the stairs.

"I'll go." Audrey whisked past their aunt while Tessa continued to stare at her older sister, whose shoulders fell.

Suddenly feeling sorry for the woman who'd seemed lost since their father's death, Tessa reached for her hand. "Meredith, even Dad couldn't protect us from everything. Mom still died. So did Nick." And Meredith had lost her joy when he'd forced her to give away the baby she'd begged him to let her keep.

Lifting her gaze to Tessa's once again, Meredith said, "I guess you want me to apologize to Dirk."

"No. I think I'd prefer to smooth things over myself."

Though how she would do that exactly plagued her thoughts all through church and lunch. Not to mention how she'd manage to break away without the boys.

When her sisters departed for their own homes after lunch, Tessa changed clothes and came back downstairs to find a foil-wrapped package on the table.

"What's this?" She looked at her aunt, who was wiping down the old, chipped counters.

"Barbecue meat left over from the party."

"Are you going to freeze it?"

Shaking her head, Aunt Dee turned on the faucet to rinse her rag. "It's for you to take to Dirk." Then, before Tessa could respond, she hollered, "Boys, get your swim trunks on. We're goin' to the swimmin' hole."

The cheers were instantaneous as they raced through the kitchen, into the hall and up the stairs.

"But I don't even know if he's home," she told a smiling Dee.

"Then call him." Tossing the rag aside, she perched her fists on her hips. "Though I s'pect you don't want to do that. The element of surprise would probably be better."

"But—"

Her aunt held up a hand, cutting her off. "Tessa, you know you want to. So stop second-guessin' yourself and go."

After saying goodbye to the boys and telling them she had an errand to run, she drove to Dirk's. Following the winding road through the Black Angus dotted pastures of his parents' ranch, she hoped they didn't mind her showing up uninvited.

As she contemplated this morning, a part of her still wanted to wring Meredith's neck. Dirk was a good guy. Humble. Kind. Sensitive to the needs of others. All packaged in one extraordinarily handsome package.

Discarding that last thought, she wished her sister had come to her with her concerns instead of trying to take on the role of their father. Especially since he was the reason Meredith was who she was, instead of the woman God intended her to be.

Under a cloudless sky, Tessa pulled up to Dirk's house, noting that his truck was nowhere in sight. Perhaps it was in the garage. Did he have a garage? Only one way to find out.

She turned off her vehicle, drawing in a bolstering breath as she grabbed the plate of barbecue and opened her door to step into the scorching midafternoon air. Moments later, she knocked on the door but was met with silence. Like a nosy neighbor, she lifted her sunglasses to peer through the glass but found no Dirk. Maybe he was in his shop. But a tentative peek revealed it, too, was empty.

Disappointment wormed through her as she returned to her vehicle. Now what?

Setting the plate on the passenger seat once again, she started the engine, cranked the AC along with some praise and worship music and started back the way she'd come. Halfway to the entrance, she saw another vehicle pulling in. A white truck. Just like Dirk's. Was it him, though? White pickups were very common around these parts. What if it was his father or brother?

As the two vehicles closed in on each other on the single-lane drive, the truck slowed and eased to one side, affording her the right of way. Yet as they neared, she recognized Dirk behind the wheel.

Rolling down her window, she came to a stop beside him.

He did the same, his expression as curious as it was guarded. "What are you doing here?"

From the passenger seat, a panting Molly eyed Tessa.

"I came to see you." Whether it was the heat or nerves, she began to sweat. "We need to talk."

He stared out the windshield, his jaw pulsing.

Making her even more annoyed with her sister. "Please, Dirk."

Without another word, he motioned for her to follow him, and she gratefully—not to mention nervously—turned around and did just that.

Moments later, he pulled up to his house and was getting out of his truck when she eased her SUV beside it. Again, she emerged into the heat carrying the plate of meat to join him and his dog at the front bumper of the truck.

Through her sunglasses, she studied him a moment. The way his eyebrows drew together, the rigid set of his shoulders.

"Where are the boys?" he finally asked.

"Aunt Dee took them to the swimming hole. And told me to bring you this." She shoved the foil-wrapped plate toward him.

"What is it?"

"Barbecue."

"That explains why Molly's got her nose in the air."

Tessa gave the dog a quick rub. "I'm sure he'll share some with you, sweetie." Not wanting to drag out the agony, she faced Dirk again. "I heard what Meredith did. About the warning she gave you."

His jaw pulsed, but he remained silent.

"She was out of line, and I let her know it. She had no business confronting you like that. I guess, now that our dad is gone, she thinks it's her job to protect me and the boys. But her reasons were unfounded." She brushed the hair away from her face, tucking it behind her ear. "So I'm begging you, please, don't make me and my boys suffer because of Meredith's ignorance. Not only do I value our friendship, it's because of you I have my son back."

His gaze roamed the horizon for a moment before landing on her. "It's hot out here. Care to come inside?" The relieved smile on his face said more than his words ever could. And she was fairly certain she wore the same expression.

With Ms. D'Lynn's cabin completed and details for the bunkhouse still falling into place, Dirk spent the bulk of his time in his shop over the next few days, putting the finishing touches on a custom cabinet order that wasn't due to be delivered for a couple of weeks. Since he was an early riser, he typically spent a couple of hours in his workshop each morning, working on special orders prior to leaving for a job site. But with the bunkhouse—and, perhaps, the barn—looming on the horizon, he wanted to go ahead and complete the order while he had the time to spare.

Then at the end of his workday, he'd head off to Legacy Ranch to spend some time with Tessa and her boys. With Ms. D'Lynn's big shindig behind them, Tessa had been eager to get started on the dining room, so he'd helped her remove the trim and paneling, not to mention engaged with the boys. Though all they seemed to talk about was the new superhero movie, *Hero Squad: Battle for Tomorrow*.

Still holding the sprayer nozzle, he inspected the freshly lacquered cabinet doors Wednesday afternoon, admiring the character of the spalted maple. The unique wood was one of his favorites.

When his phone rang, he set the sprayer aside and stepped out of the spray booth to continue across the concrete floor. Passing Molly, he removed his respirator to inhale the earthy scent of wood as he glanced at the screen.

The sight of his mother-in-law's name had an invisible weight settling on his chest. It was rare that he spoke with Meg or her husband, Doyle, these days. Though they lived little more than an hour and a half away, outside of Austin, any reconnecting seemed to take place only around the holidays. Even then, the calls were more obligatory than anything. Since Lindsey had two siblings and together they'd given their parents five grandchildren, there was really no reason for them to stay in contact with him anymore.

So why was Meg calling him today? Was there something wrong with her or Doyle?

Molly stood and moved beside him as he continued across the shop. When he finally tapped the screen and set the device to his ear, his other hand instinctively fell to Molly.

"Hello."

"Dirk." Meg dragged his name out. "It's so good to hear your voice. Did I catch you at a bad time?"

He peered up at the barn's rafters, willing himself to sound normal. Engaged even. "No, you're good. What's up?"

"I was thinking about you, so I thought I'd give you a call."

He couldn't help smiling. Meg was a lovely, outgoing person who put others before herself. "Thank you, Meg. I appreciate that." Lowering his gaze to peer out the window, he watched the cattle grazing in the pasture just over the fence. "How's the family?"

"Good. The kids are growing." She cleared her throat, as though second-guessing her comment. "What about you? What are you up to?"

He filled her in on what he'd been doing workwise. Because until lately, he hadn't had much of a life outside of his work. Not until Tessa and the boys arrived at Legacy Ranch.

"It sounds like the Lord is presenting you with some wonderful opportunities."

"Yes, ma'am, He certainly is." Images of Tessa, Grayson and Bryce played across his mind, though he quickly dismissed them. It didn't seem right to be thinking of them while he was talking with his late wife's mother.

"I am so pleased to hear that." After a brief pause, she said, "I know this is none of my business, but by chance are you seeing anyone?"

His cheeks heated. "No, ma'am. I pretty much keep to myself." Well, until Tessa and her boys came along, anyway.

He reached for Molly. His life had been fuller these last six weeks than at any time since the accident. But unless Tessa got that teaching position, they'd be going back to Houston in a few weeks and his life would go back to the way it had been before. And that depressed him far more than it should.

"Dirk," Meg said matter-of-factly, "you were a wonderful husband and father. Doyle and I couldn't have handpicked a better mate for Lindsey or daddy for Emory. But it's okay for you to find happiness with someone else. I mean, if you were gone, wouldn't you want the same for Lindsey?"

He dropped into the camp chair he kept in his shop, allowing Molly to rest her chin in his lap. Of course, he would. Lindsey was a beautiful woman, inside and out. And she had so much love to give.

Feeling more than a little uncomfortable, he cleared his throat. "Yes, ma'am, I would." But then, Lindsey wasn't the one responsible for the accident.

Molly whined, licking his free hand.

"Stop blaming yourself, Dirk."

How did she know?

"The accident was not your fault. I know you don't want to believe that, but it's true. God spared you for a reason. And it wasn't for you to hide away from the world. It's time for you to accept the past and embrace the future God has for you."

Suddenly Tessa and her boys appeared in his mind's eye. Could they be his future?

Shaking off the notion, he said, "Meg, it's good to know that you're still not afraid to pull any punches."

She chuckled. "Oh, I love you, Dirk. And I want nothing but the best for you."

When the call ended, Dirk was surprised how much lighter he felt. And his thoughts immediately turned to Tessa.

Until Meredith had ambushed him Saturday afternoon, he'd been feeling pretty good about their relationship. Then suddenly he was second-guessing his actions and motives. Initially, they'd been all about Grayson and helping him. Dirk genuinely cared about the kid. Both him and his brother. Yet the more he and Tessa got to know one another and discovered how much they had in common, the deeper their friendship grew. But had it moved beyond friendship?

He'd been miserable when he left Ms. D'Lynn's Saturday. Until Tessa showed up here Sunday, making him smile again. Why was that?

Because he and Tessa were more than friends. They'd connected over some of the deepest, darkest moments of their lives. They could be real with one another. There was no need to sugarcoat their questions or responses. They were able to be honest without having to worry what the other might think. Something many married couples couldn't do. Tessa had unlocked something he'd kept bottled up.

Looking back, he now realized Meredith had only wanted to protect Tessa and her sons. But he shouldn't have allowed her to get to him. Because if that turn of events had proven anything, it was how much he'd grown to care for the pretty teacher and her two boys. Far more than he'd been willing to admit.

"Come on, Molly." Dirk stood and started toward the back door. "Let's get some fresh air."

Outside, the warm breeze cleared the cobwebs from his mind as he breathed in the scent of fresh air and sunshine. Once he finished lacquering the rest of the cabinets, he'd head to Ms. D'Lynn's and maybe play a game of cornhole with Grayson and Bryce before helping Tessa in the dining room.

His phone signaled a text. He hoped it was a quote from one of the subcontractors he'd been waiting on.

Instead, he saw Tessa's name on the screen. Beneath it, the words, I have an interview Friday, were followed by a trio of smiley face emojis.

As he stood there wearing the same expression, Meg's words played through his mind. *It's time for you to accept the past and embrace the future God has for you.*

Was it possible that Tessa could be a part of that future?

# Chapter Twelve

❦

"Aunt Dee, I think we have shopped till I'm about to drop." Tessa closed the door at the log cabin late Saturday afternoon, not wanting to let the cool air from the mini split escape, then deposited the last of the shopping bags that had filled the cargo area of her SUV onto the old wood floor that now boasted a new satin finish.

"I hear ya, sister." Standing at the kitchen counter, already unpacking the first round of bags, her aunt smiled. "But I can't wait to start puttin' this place together."

In addition to kitchen, bath and decor items they'd picked up today, they'd purchased a sofa sleeper and a cozy chair for the living space, along with a vintage-style metal bedframe with a mattress and box spring for the loft, but those items wouldn't be delivered until Monday.

Swiping the back of her hand across her damp brow, she watched Dee pull item after item from shopping bags, while grinning like a kid on Christmas morning. It did Tessa good to see her aunt so happy. But how sad was it that her sixty-two-year-old aunt was faring better than her? At least their shopping spree had kept Tessa from dwelling on her interview yesterday. The one that went really well, and she prayed would pan out. Except she wasn't the only candidate. And they'd seemed concerned about the fact that she lived in

Houston, despite her telling them she was prepared to move to the area.

"I don't know that I have the energy today. I'm about give out." As her grandmother used to say. "And I still need to go get the boys." Dirk had offered to take them to see that new superhero movie in Brenham and then back to his house until she returned. Though he probably hadn't anticipated her being gone so long. She hadn't, either. But when Aunt Dee was on a mission, there was no stopping her.

She joined her aunt in the kitchen, once again admiring the rustic cabinets Dirk had made. He sure had done a good job of staying true to the character of this cabin. "I'm sure Dirk hadn't planned on keeping them this long."

Pausing, her aunt looked at her. "You're sweet on him, aren't you?"

Tessa shook her head. Between her aunt and her mother-in-law… "Aw, come on, Aunt Dee, don't do that to me."

"Do what? State the obvious?" She wagged a finger, those blue eyes of hers boring into Tessa's. "You forget how well I know you. I've been watchin' the two of you all these weeks. You've become great friends, and I couldn't be more tickled about that. You understand each other." One hand perched on her hip, the woman continued to stare. "And that's taken your relationship to another level."

"Yes… However, it doesn't mean—"

"Or maybe it does." With a wink, her aunt returned to the task at hand.

More than eager to escape, Tessa said, "Since I'll be taking my car to get the boys—" she gestured outside the door "—would you like me to run to the house and bring you the utility vehicle or your truck?" As if she'd be running anywhere.

"Nah." Her aunt waved her off. "I'll just walk."

How sad was it that her aunt had more energy than she did? Evidently pulling nails from shiplap didn't do much for one's stamina.

"Alright, then, we'll see you at the house later." With a wave, Tessa continued out the door into the humid air. Then texted Dirk to let him know she was on her way.

Before she started the engine, he responded, telling her to come to his shop.

During the fifteen-minute drive, she contemplated what to feed the boys for supper. What she wouldn't give for a fast-food restaurant. But she'd have to drive back to Brenham for that.

That was one big adjustment she'd have to get used to if they moved to Legacy Ranch. In Houston, they had virtually every kind of fast food just up the road. But then, if her boys were happier—and, by default, herself—she supposed she could live with that.

Tightening her grip on the steering wheel as she traversed the slow rolling hills, she said, "God, You worked a miracle with Dan and Gina. And, in turn, Grayson. So, Lord, if it's possible—" She shook her head. "I mean, if it's Your will—" Why was that part so hard to pray?

*Because you want your will, not His.*

"If it's in Your will, I pray that You would make a way for me and the boys to move out here." Crossing the cattle guard at Dirk's family ranch, she added an "Amen."

Minutes later, she neared Dirk's house, once again marveling at the modern-looking structure. He definitely had a gift. To be able to look at something old and run-down and see its potential.

That had her thinking about the old barn at Legacy Ranch. Or more to the point, all the ideas her sisters had bandied regarding its use. And while she found herself partial to the idea of a venue, the glaring objection was who would manage the thing once it was up and running. That is, if it was even big enough to be used for something like that. Perhaps she'd have to get Dirk to walk her through it one day.

She parked, admiring the twin crepe myrtles on either side of the walkway leading to the front door. Their white flowers were a nice contrast to the dark metal siding.

Outside, the skirt of her sundress swayed in the breeze that offered nary a morsel of relief from the ninety-plus degree heat. Per Dirk's instructions, she followed the gravel path to the far end of the structure where his shop was. Approaching the door, she heard her boys giggling inside.

Her heart swelled with appreciation. There had been many times these last few years when she'd wondered if they'd ever laugh again. Life had become a drudgery, especially this last year. Going through the motions, sometimes struggling to get through each day.

Until Dirk came along with his seemingly unending patience and faith-filled perspective of life. He'd challenged her and made her look at things differently.

And after all he'd been through.

"Knock, knock," she said as she opened the door, scanning what had to be the cleanest woodworking shop ever. One would be hard-pressed to find even a speck of sawdust, though the aroma of wood still filled in the air.

Molly trotted toward her, ears perked, and Tessa rubbed the soft fur atop her head.

"Mama, look what I made." Bryce held up a partially painted birdhouse in shades of red and blue as she approached.

"Wow." Pausing beside them, she smoothed a hand over her youngest son's messy hair. "Looks like you guys have been busy. How was the movie?"

"It was *awesome*." To see Grayson's dark eyes sparkle as he ticked off all the high points did her heart good. And it was all because the man beside him had cared enough to look past her son's moodiness and create a safe environment where Grayson felt comfortable opening up.

Her appreciative gaze lifted to Dirk as her son went on. What a wonderful father he must've been. He was so patient. She eyed the paint on the work bench then. Not to mention brave.

Because of him, they weren't the same family who'd arrived at Legacy Ranch a little over six weeks ago. They laughed now. And she'd noticed Dirk smiling more, too. Making the already handsome man even more attractive.

*You understand each other. And that's taken your relationship to another level.*

While Tessa wanted to discount her aunt's comment, she knew it was true. Still, if she wasn't offered the teaching position, she and the boys would be going back to Houston. And, at the moment, that made her very sad.

"How did the shopping go?" Dirk looked her way, a smile lighting those gray-blue eyes of his, and nearly knocking her off her feet. This may be the first time his smile had truly reached his eyes. And the things it did to her heart were best not dwelled on right now.

"Good. I think we got most everything on Aunt Dee's list. The furniture will be delivered Monday. However, I am exhausted." She looked at her boys. "Which means we'd better go because I still have to fix supper." Although she was leaning heavily toward frozen pizza.

As her boys groaned, Dirk said, "Well, if you don't have anything planned, you all are welcome to have supper with me. I'm making spaghetti, so there'll be plenty to share."

"Can we, Mom?" Grayson's eyes were wide with anticipation.

"Please." His brother clasped his hands together.

She couldn't blame them. Spending the evening with Dirk was pretty appealing to her, too. Despite the warning bells going off in her mind.

"You know what?" She smiled Dirk's way. "I think I would like that very much. Spaghetti sounds *really* good." Not to mention an evening with her handsome friend.

After spending much of Wednesday clearing out the bunkhouse, Dirk had dropped off Grayson before heading home for a quick shower and change of clothes. It sure felt good having his little buddy with him again. Even made the July heat tolerable. That and an industrial fan he'd brought from his shop.

Since Ms. D'Lynn and her nieces had approved of the changes he'd made to the design, he'd been as eager to get started as Ms. D'Lynn was. There was just something about old buildings that spoke to him and drew him in. Even though the bunkhouse was essentially a blank canvas, somewhere within it lay a personality as unique as the building itself.

The log cabin, for instance, was rugged, with a hint of femininity. The barn that was now his home represented hardworking, forward-thinking people, something he felt he'd captured in his design. He could hardly wait to get a better feel for the bunkhouse.

Now as he maneuvered his truck over the cattle guard at Legacy Ranch to continue up the long drive to Ms. D'Lynn's, he patted Molly.

"What do you say, girl? Are you ready for another evening of supper and adventures in shiplap?"

Tongue dangling, she seemed to smile his way.

Something was different, though. There was lightness about him.

He couldn't remember the last time he'd felt this way.

Certainly not since the accident.

*It's time for you to accept the past and embrace the future God has for you.*

With Meg's words replaying in his mind, he glanced out over the pasture, recalling a verse in First Peter that talked about suffering and God's restoration. Did he dare hope for something more than friendship with Tessa? What if she didn't get the position at the school?

*Houston isn't that far away.*

A smile tugged at the corner of his mouth.

When he reached the ranch house, the boys were on the porch. And they were wearing swimsuits.

Hmm. Had he missed that memo?

He parked and stepped out of the truck with Molly on his heels. Then they continued toward the porch to greet the boys.

They'd just reached the steps when Tessa appeared at the door.

"There you are." Wearing tan shorts and a black tank top, she looked at her boys. "If you want Aunt Dee to take you two to the swimming hole, you'd best come inside and eat."

With a gasp, the duo scurried into the house.

Dirk stopped beside her on the porch. "Guess that means we're not included in that little outing." Just as well since he hadn't brought any swim trunks. He might need to start keeping a pair in his truck.

"No. However, I do have something else planned." She seemed to catch herself. "That is, if you're agreeable to it."

Looking into her eyes with those flecks of gold, he was apt to agree to anything. "What do you want me to agree to?"

"Could we go down to the old barn after supper?"

"Sure. Is there a problem?"

"No." Looking away, she said, "I've just been thinking about it since my sisters were here. They're throwing out all these ideas and I'm just not getting it, so I'd like to have another look. And since the boys will be gone, I thought this might be a good opportunity."

"Yeah, you got it." His stomach growled. "Please tell me we can eat first, though. I'm starving."

She shook her head, sending those pretty waves of hers bouncing back and forth. And making him wonder what they might feel like. "You're as bad as my boys."

Grayson and Bryce wasted no time scarfing down their supper. Evidently, swimming was a good motivator. Once they were gone, Dirk, Tessa and Molly piled into his truck and drove to the barn.

While Molly followed him out of the truck into the heat, Dirk found himself wishing he was with the boys instead of hanging out inside a hot, dusty, barn. Then again, the company was definitely a draw.

"Oh, *wow*." Tessa tossed the passenger door closed, her gaze fixed just beyond the barn.

The awe in her voice had him turning. The sun was glimmering off of the pond back there, casting a golden glow across the landscape.

"That is gorgeous." She eyed him as he joined her at the front bumper.

Pulling out his phone, he said, "Definitely photograph worthy." He took a couple of shots while Tessa did the same with her phone. "That's the kind of thing you'd want to put on a website. Well, depending on what you ladies decide to do with this place."

"My sisters are still talking about a venue." Her thumbs

danced across her screen before returning the phone to her back pocket. "I sent them a picture."

"I take it you're not in agreement with them. About the venue, I mean."

"After seeing your place, I have a little better understanding of where they're coming from. But I'd like to take a look at the *guts*—as you call them. Maybe you could walk me through things."

"In that case, let's go check it out."

Inside, the sun peered through gaps in the wood siding, affording them a fair amount of light that highlighted the dust particles hovering in the air.

With Molly on his left and Tessa to his right, Dirk paused beside a post.

"Like I've mentioned before, the structural posts are the heart of the barn." He rested his palm on it, the hand-hewn wood smooth beneath his fingers. "The exterior walls will come down, and the roof removed."

"So it'll be a skeleton."

"That's a good way to put it. So all of the area you see right now within these four walls would be your starting point. Like, if you did a venue, this would be your main area. Then, you could add wings onto each side for things like a kitchen, dressing rooms, bathrooms." Retrieving his phone, he added, "Like this." Pulling up an image, he showed it to her.

"Okay, now I get it." She smiled. "That makes a lot more sense." She smoothed a hand over one of the posts, her appreciative gaze roving from bottom to top and back. "These posts do look really cool. Lots of character." She glanced his way. "We could call it The Barn at Legacy Ranch."

"Uh-oh. Sounds like you've caught your sisters' vision."

With a grin, she said, "I think so, too." Her eyes sparkled. "Thank you for so patiently walking me through the process."

"You're welcome." For some unknown reason he held out his hand. "Shall we go outside for some fresh air?"

"Yes, please." Then, as if it was the most natural thing in the world, she placed her hand in his.

"Come on, Molly." His heart was pounding like a bass drum by the time they neared his truck. And that glow on the pond was ever more stunning.

Yet it paled in comparison to the woman holding his hand.

Looking out over the water, Tessa sighed. "This is so beautiful."

"It sure is." Except he wasn't talking about the pond.

As if realizing he was watching her, she looked up at him.

He cupped her cheek with his hand, reveling in the softness of her skin as his fingers threaded into her silky hair. And he was more than pleased when she didn't pull away. Then, before he could second-guess himself, he lowered his lips to hers.

His hopes soared when she responded. He wasn't sure how long they remained connected, nor did he care. And when they finally parted, all he could do was stare into her beautiful eyes.

With his thumb still caressing her cheek, he said, "You have no idea how long I've thought about doing that."

A smile played at her lips. "So why didn't you?"

"Well, two curious little boys and an aunt who's even more so, for starters."

Her soft laughter washed over him.

"Actually, I was going to wait until you heard back about the teaching position, but we're alone and the opportunity was too hard to resist." He finally lowered his hand, only to take hold of hers.

"And? Was it worth it?" He loved the teasing lilt in her voice.

"I think so. But just to be sure…" He kissed her again.

This time when they parted, she sighed, resting her forehead against his chest. "Dirk, what if I don't get the job?"

"We can find a way to make things work. Houston isn't that far away."

"I know, but once school starts and I'm working full-time, juggling the boys' activities, I won't be able to come out here very often."

"Then I'll come to you."

Shaking her head, she stepped away. "I spent a good part of my marriage in a long-distance relationship."

He swallowed the sudden lump in his throat. "So, does this mean we're over before we even start?"

She looked at him. "That makes me sad just thinking about it."

He dared a step closer. "You know, Hope Crossing isn't the only school district around here. What if there's another position somewhere else in the area?"

"I hadn't considered that."

"Will you?"

Her smile gave him hope. "Given how eager my boys are to move out here, yes. I think that's a spectacular idea."

He couldn't agree more.

# Chapter Thirteen

Two days later, the memory of Dirk's kiss was every bit as fresh and indescribably wonderful as it had been Wednesday night. Tessa hadn't been kissed in so long, she wasn't sure she'd know how to respond. Thankfully, there were some things that were intuitive.

In Dirk's embrace, she'd felt wanted. And his kiss had been fraught with promise. A promise she longed to embrace. But Nick had made promises, too. Then abandoned her and their sons.

Except Dirk knew the pain of loss, too, and it had taught him how fragile and precious relationships were. And that they shouldn't be taken for granted.

Wednesday's momentous event had her diving wholeheartedly into finishing the dining room. Now that she knew how to tackle the task like a pro, the project was moving along much faster than the living room had. And she couldn't wait to complete it, so she'd have time to enjoy the revived space before they had to go back to Houston.

*If* they went back to Houston.

She wiped the sweat from her brow with the back of her hand, recalling the promise she'd made to Dirk to check for openings at other school districts in the area. Yet she'd been so engrossed in the shiplap, she'd all but forgotten.

So as eleven thirty approached, she set her paintbrush aside and went into the kitchen to grab a mini can of Dr Pepper from the refrigerator. Setting it on the butcher-block island, she popped the top and took a sip, glimpsing her laptop on the table. With Bryce playing at Owen's house, Grayson at the bunkhouse with Dirk and her aunt doing who knows what around the ranch, this would be as good a time as any for her to follow through on that promise.

Moving to the table, she slipped into a chair and opened the computer, glancing toward the antique schoolhouse clock on the wall, its pendulum ticking out a rhythm as it swayed back and forth. Once the laptop booted, she pulled up the district website for Brenham, knowing it was the largest in the area—albeit much smaller than what she was used to—making openings more likely. After navigating to the employment postings, she noticed the first one was for an elementary school teacher. Her cursor hovered over the Apply button. Until she heard her phone ringing in the dining room.

Standing, she hurried to catch it before it went to voicemail, barely noting the number on the screen.

"Hello."

"Is this Tessa Wagner?"

"Yes, it is."

"Hello, Tessa. This is Bethany Wilks, the principal at Hope Crossing elementary school. We spoke last week."

"Yes, ma'am. How are you?" Tessa attempted to sound nonchalant, but with her heart racing, she wasn't sure she'd pulled it off.

"I'm doing well, thank you. I am calling to let you know how much I enjoyed meeting with you last week, and to offer you the second-grade teaching position we discussed."

Tessa didn't know if she was going to laugh or cry. "That is wonderful news. Thank you, so much."

"I think you're going to be a great addition to our team, and I'm looking forward to working with you."

"Likewise."

"I'll send over your contract via email shortly. Once you get everything filled out, you can drop the paperwork off at the human resources office, which is in the admin building by the high school."

"Got it. Thank you so much." Tessa ended the call, feeling as though she might explode. Breaking into an impromptu happy dance, she tried to recall the last time she'd been so genuinely happy.

Dirk's kiss came to mind. No doubt about it, that was a pretty spectacular kiss. But this was a different kind of happy. This was life-changing for her and her boys.

*And that kiss wasn't?*

Not in the immediate future.

She looked around the house that she would soon call home. "I can't believe we actually get to live here."

*Thank You, God.*

Her mind drifted back to the day they arrived at Legacy Ranch. The plea that had been on her lips. *God, please let this summer make a difference in Grayson's life. In all our lives.*

"Lord, I never could've imagined what You had in store for us. We've found healing. And so much more." Her faith had grown. And she had Dirk to thank for that.

Hearing Aunt Dee's truck rolling up the drive, Tessa hurried through the kitchen to the laundry room and burst out onto the carriage porch as her aunt emerged from the pickup with Nash.

"Guess what?" It had been ages since Tessa had smiled like this. Her cheeks actually hurt.

Her aunt joined her on the porch, grinning. "Well, if the

smile on your face is any indication, it's somethin' pretty special."

"The school called. They offered me the position."

"Oh, darlin'." Uncharacteristic tears shimmered in her aunt's blue eyes before she wrapped her arms around Tessa. "That is wonderful news." Releasing her, she swept away an errant tear. "Have you told the boys? Dirk?"

Tessa shook her head. "I haven't had time. I just got off the phone as you were pulling in." She brushed the hair away from her face, worrying her bottom lip. "Do you realize how much there is to do between now and when school starts— in less than three weeks?" The realization had a wave of panic washing over her. "Not the least of which is our house in Houston."

"Audrey said she'd help you with that."

"I know, but that's just the tip of the iceberg. There's so much more to do." She'd have to get the boys' school transcripts, have their mail forwarded, pack up their clothes and everything else in their house! "I'd better start making a list."

"When are you gonna tell the boys? And Dirk?"

"I don't know." She wanted to hop in the utility vehicle and hurry down to the bunkhouse to tell Dirk. But Grayson was there, and she'd rather tell the boys when they were together.

Nash barked then and took off toward the entry hall.

"I'm ho-ome." Grayson's voice had Tessa starting that way.

Standing in the opening between the kitchen and entry hall, she said, "What are you two doing here?"

"Calling it a day," a sweaty Dirk said as Grayson whisked past her, his own hair wet with sweat.

"Yeah, y'all don't need to be in that bunkhouse past lunchtime," Aunt Dee said behind her. "Not when they're callin' for triple digits."

In the kitchen now, Dirk eyed Tessa. "Thought I'd help you in the dining room this afternoon."

"Oh." Running her fingers over Molly's soft fur, Tessa pulled her bottom lip between her teeth, realizing she'd all but forgotten about the project since that phone call.

Dirk narrowed his gaze. "Are you alright? You seem—I don't know—flustered."

She waved him off. "I've just got a lot on my mind." And it was increasing by the second. Right along with her blood pressure. What had she gotten herself into?

Molly pressed against her leg.

And when Dirk noticed, he lifted a brow. "Is there something you'd care to discuss?"

While she was eager to share her news with him, she couldn't do it with Grayson standing right there.

"Hey, Grayson," Dee started, "why don't you grab a fresh shirt from the laundry room, and we'll run into Hope Crossing to pick up some more ice cream."

"Sure!" He wasted no time complying. And before Tessa knew it, they were gone.

Hands on his hips, Dirk glared at her, his focus bouncing between her and Molly. "Why do I get the feeling your aunt hadn't really been planning a trip to the store?"

"You're very perceptive."

He nodded slowly. "And so is Molly. She's been clinging to you since we got here. What's going on?"

A nervous laugh escaped her lips as he stopped in front of her, his T-shirt still damp with sweat. Even sweaty, he was attractive.

Peering up at him, she said, "You're looking at Hope Crossing's new second-grade teacher."

A slow smile started building behind that beard of his. "You got the job?"

"Mmm-hmm." She nodded, still trying to wrap her own brain around the news. "I don't want to tell the boys until they're together, though, so mum's the word."

"This is great news, right?"

"I think so."

"Then why are you so on edge? Isn't this what you wanted?"

"Yes. But after I got off the phone I started thinking about all the things moving out here is going to entail. And school starts in less than three weeks." Holding up a hand, she started ticking things off on her fingers. "We'll need to pack up all of our household goods, find someplace to store them." Her voice seemed to climb an octave with each syllable. "I don't even know where to begin."

Palming the back of her neck, he drew her closer and pressed his lips to hers. And for the briefest of moments, she forgot whatever it was she'd been ranting over.

Then he pulled away, those gray-blue eyes fixed on hers. "Now tell me, how I can help you?"

"Is this the place?" Dirk eased his pickup truck alongside the curb in front of the single-story home with a brown brick and Texas fieldstone facade just after eight the next morning.

"Yes, sir." The dual response came from the back seat, where Grayson and Bryce sat with Molly in between them. They'd certainly made the trip to Houston much more entertaining than if Dirk had driven it alone. Meanwhile, Tessa was able to have a little solitude as she, no doubt, contemplated the task ahead. Either that or she'd been on the phone with one or more of her sisters.

Once Tessa had calmed down yesterday, they'd decided to make the drive to her home this morning and spend the day gathering whatever immediate items she and the boys wanted to take back to Legacy Ranch.

Now he checked his mirrors to make sure the cargo trailer he typically used for transporting cabinets or wood furniture wasn't blocking the driveway, then turned off the engine.

As soon as the doors unlocked, Grayson bolted from the vehicle.

"Wait for me." Bryce unhooked from his booster seat to follow his brother without even bothering to close the door.

Smiling, Dirk shook his head, recalling similar competitions between him and Jared when they were kids.

He stepped from the vehicle, the oppressive Houston humidity descending on him as he tossed the door closed and continued around to the other side. At the wide-open back door, he signaled for Molly to join him, then attached a handle to her vest as she watched after the boys.

"You're growing kind of fond of those two, aren't you?" He gave Molly a pat. "Yeah, me, too." Their mama, in particular.

He closed the door and started toward the driveway as the double garage door ascended, revealing everything from Christmas decorations to bicycles, lawn equipment and toys. Kind of reminded him of his and Lindsey's house in Austin.

They'd stored so much in the two-car garage, there was barely room for one vehicle. Of course, he'd gotten rid of most of it. What good were bicycles when there was no one to ride them?

He tucked the memories away, glad he was able to be here to help Tessa. Though the decision hadn't been without some trepidation. Audrey wasn't the only one Tessa had talked with in the last twenty-four hours. She'd been on the phone with Meredith, too. And after what had transpired the last time he'd seen Tessa's eldest sister... Even if she had apologized via Tessa, seeing Meredith again was bound to be awkward. So he was relieved when Tessa told him Meredith had a previous engagement and wouldn't be here today.

One hand in the pocket of his cargo shorts, he paused beside Tessa and the boys. "Nice place you've got here." The modest neighborhood couldn't be more than five years old. Dirk couldn't help noticing how close together the homes were. Something he'd gotten used to living in Austin. Though after growing up on a ranch, it had taken some time.

"Thank you. I've always liked it." Dressed for comfort in shorts and a tee, Tessa turned her attention to her sons. "I just got off the phone with Aunt Audrey. She's on her way with coffee and donuts."

The boys gave a collective gasp. Meanwhile Dirk was jazzed about the coffee. He'd regretted not bringing his thermos.

"Did you boys behave for Mr. Dirk?" While the question was for her sons, her gaze was on Dirk.

"Yes, ma'am."

"They did fine," he assured her.

She took a deep breath, her shoulders rising and falling with the effort. "I guess we may as well go inside."

While the boys rushed into the garage, Dirk poked a thumb over his shoulder as he addressed Tessa. "Do you want me to get the boxes and storage containers out of the trailer?"

"Why don't I show you around first."

"In that case, lead the way."

Inside the tastefully decorated home, she adjusted the thermostat on the air conditioning before walking him through the three-bedroom, two-bath space with light greige walls and gray vinyl plank flooring throughout. Grayson and Bryce proudly showed him their rooms, too.

"Coffee's here!" Audrey hollered as they finished.

"And donuts?" Grayson bounded into the kitchen that had white cabinetry and a subway tile backsplash, gray granite countertops and stainless-steel appliances.

"And donuts." Audrey eyed Tessa and Dirk as they approached. "There are some breakfast sandwiches, too, for anyone who'd like a little protein."

After downing a sandwich, a couple of donut holes and a cup and a half of coffee, Dirk had the boys follow him to the trailer. In part to help him unload, but also to give Tessa and her sister some time to discuss Tessa's plans, fluid as they were.

Then while Tessa and Audrey set to work in Tessa's bedroom at one end of the house, Dirk helped the boys with their rooms on the opposite side. Molly parked herself in the short hallway where she could keep a watchful eye on both boys.

"Clothes and footwear first," Dirk instructed.

"What about our toys?" In Bryce's room, the wide-eyed boy gaped up at him.

"We'll get to those later. First we need to get everything from your drawers and whatever's hanging in your closet."

As the boy set to work, Dirk noticed a five-by-seven framed photo atop the dresser. A man wearing a desert camouflage uniform and a big smile held a little boy that couldn't have been more than three years old. "Is this you and your dad?" Dirk pointed.

Bryce nodded. "I was just little." He continued pulling socks and underwear from a bottom drawer. "I don't remember it."

Dirk's heart went out to the boy. Bryce had been four when his daddy left them. The same age Emory was when Dirk lost her.

Dropping to one knee, he said, "Do you have memories of your dad?"

Molly joined them then, plopping down beside Bryce.

The boy shrugged. "Kinda. I remember riding on his shoulders, pretending he was a horsey."

"My dad used to do that with me, too. I bet you had fun."

Bryce stared at Molly. "Yeah."

"Should we take our coats and jackets?"

Dirk looked up to find Grayson standing in the doorway, holding a windbreaker in one hand and a fleece jacket in the other.

Dirk stood. "You won't need either of those for a while, but you will need them eventually, so I would say yes." But then, after hearing Tessa's comments about how fast Grayson was growing, they might not fit him anymore. "Double-check with your mom, though."

As storage containers were filled over the next few hours, Dirk labeled and hauled them to the garage where they were stacked. Making him glad he'd thought to bring a dolly. But then, in his experience, when women were packing, it was best to plan for extra. Not that he'd ever say that in front of Tessa or her sisters.

"What's for lunch?" Grayson added a lid to one of his boxes a little before noon.

Dirk shrugged. "I don't know if your mom and aunt have any plans or not."

"We should order pizza." Bryce came up behind Dirk.

Ah, the joy of pizza delivery. Something that wasn't available in the country. "Sounds good to me. Let's run it past your mom and aunt and see what they say."

With his mouth already watering at the prospect, Dirk was pleased when the women agreed. And since Audrey had an app on her phone, she went ahead and placed the order. Then sputtered when Dirk handed her the cash to cover the cost.

"They're saying it should be here in thirty to forty minutes." Audrey tucked her phone in the back pocket of her shorts.

"Good deal. That'll give the boys time to start going through their toys."

"This container's ready if you'd like to take it." Tessa pointed to the large bin full of shoes.

He looked from the container to Tessa. "Do you actually wear all of those?"

Looking rather indignant—in a cute sort of way—she said, "Not at the same time, but yes, I do."

"O-kay." He hoisted the clear plastic container into his arms, making a mental note that Tessa was sensitive about her shoes. Then he headed to the garage with Molly at his side.

He'd just set it on the floor when he heard a car door close. Surely that wasn't the pizza already.

Turning, he saw Meredith coming into the garage.

He pulled in a long breath, his spine stiffening. *She's Tessa's sister, so be nice.*

The next thing he knew, Molly was nudging him.

"Meredith." He nodded, trying for a genuine smile.

Wearing a casual black skirt and V-neck tee, her brown hair pulled back, she looked somewhat approachable.

He poked a thumb over his shoulder. "Your sisters are in Tessa's room going through her stuff, if you'd like to join them."

"Thank you. I will do that." She cleared her throat. "But first…" She clasped her hands—tightly, by the looks of things—and stared at him. "I owe you an apology. I was out of line that day at my aunt's house. You did nothing to deserve that sort of treatment, and I hope you can forgive me."

Dirk just stood there, his mouth hanging open. "I, uh…" He rubbed the back of his neck, puffing out a chuckle. "I certainly was not expecting that."

"After our last interaction, no, I don't suppose you were. But I meant what I said."

"Oh, I believe you. It's just, uh, well…" Lowering his hand to Molly, he met Meredith's gaze. "Yes, I do accept your apology. And just so you'll know, I'm rather humbled."

"Well, then, perhaps we can start again."

"I'd like that very much." Because he cared far too much for Tessa to be at odds with anyone in her family. Not when he was starting to envision a future with the pretty widow and her two precious little boys.

# Chapter Fourteen

Dirk climbed the front porch steps at Ms. D'Lynn's the next afternoon, Molly at his side, much the way he'd done all those weeks ago after discovering Grayson at the cabin. Back then, he never would have imagined how that one moment would change his life.

"This box is heavy." Moving through the entry hall, Bryce continued up the stairway, grunting and groaning like an old man.

"Not as heavy as mine." Grayson trudged behind him.

Dirk and Molly followed the duo, Dirk toting a large storage container holding Tessa's shoes. "Sorry, fellas, I've got you both beat, so keep it moving."

Since it had been almost sunset when they'd returned from Houston last night, Dirk had unhitched his trailer and left it parked at the ranch house so they could unload after church today. Then, since the boys had pleaded with him the entire drive back to Legacy Ranch, he'd joined them at their church this morning instead of attending his regular house of worship. Something he'd rather enjoyed. Sitting in the pew with the boys between them, while he and Tessa shared surreptitious glances, had things feeling like they were a couple. A family even. A notion he kind of liked.

At the top of the stairs, the boys continued into the large

bedroom that spanned the back of the house while he and Molly rounded into the hall. Setting the box on the old wood-plank floor in Tessa's room, he heard her voice drifting up the stairs.

"That's the last one. Now all I have to do is unpack everything and find places to store all of it."

He certainly didn't envy her on that count. According to Tessa, the containers they'd brought back held all of her and the boys' clothing, footwear and outerwear. That was in addition to the boys' toys, books, bicycles and things of sentimental value. Plus whatever had been in her pantry.

Dirk returned to the hall to hear Grayson groan as he started down the steps. "I'm hot."

"Me, too," Bryce whined behind his brother.

Falling in line behind them, Dirk heard Ms. D'Lynn say, "Well, I have an idea, if y'all are interested."

Clad in denim shorts and a pink T-shirt, she eyed them as they neared the bottom of the stairs. "Y'all have been goin' and blowin' since our favorite teacher here received that wonderful phone call. Why don't you hit the pause button and we'll all head over to the swimmin' hole for a little celebration."

"Celebration?" Grayson perked up. "Does that mean there'll be cake?" The kid was always thinking about his stomach.

With a chuckle, Ms. D'Lynn shook her head. "I don't know about that, but there's a chocolate cream pie in the fridge that might do just fine."

Tessa glanced at Dirk, her smile making his heart race. Much the way it did every time he thought of her staying at Legacy Ranch for good and being able to see her every day. "What do you think?"

As long as he got to be with her... "Let's do it!"

By the time everyone else was ready, Ms. D'Lynn had an ice chest full of snacks and a beverage cooler filled with water ready to go. And as they piled into the utility vehicle, the boys were in a much better mood. Tessa sat in the front seat with Nash between her and her aunt, while the boys joined Dirk and Molly in the back seat.

Dust billowed behind the vehicle as they sped along the narrow dirt road into the woods. After bumping over a cattle guard, Ms. D'Lynn parked in the shade along the bank of the large pond. While Nash explored, Molly kept watch as Dirk and Tessa transferred the coolers to the picnic table, Grayson gathered foam noodles and an inner tube float from the bed of the utility vehicle, and Dee helped Bryce with his swim vest.

Then, once sunscreen had been applied, Ms. D'Lynn grabbed her float and eyed the boys. "You two ready?"

Grayson gathered the noodles while Bryce snagged masks and snorkels.

"Yes!"

Then, moving at a pace that was more like speed walking, the three of them started across the pier with Nash on their heels, each boy claiming they were going to be the first into the refreshing water. Meanwhile, Molly remained at Dirk's side watching after them.

Tessa shook her head. "Sometimes I think my aunt is the biggest kid of all."

"I can't say that I blame her." Dirk couldn't help grinning as he attached Molly's handle. He was pretty eager to hit the water himself. Nodding in that direction, he said, "Let's go!"

When they reached the tee in the pier, he paused at the bench to remove his prosthetic while Tessa waited. Then, hopping on his right leg while Molly flanked his left, he moved to the far edge. Looking over his shoulder, he cast Tessa a mischievous grin.

"What are you up t—" Before she finished her sentence, he launched into a cannonball.

When he surfaced, Molly was barking, apparently scolding him, while Tessa stood there dripping wet and glaring at him.

"Oh, you are in so much trouble." Jumping into the water, she began splashing him relentlessly.

"Alright, alright!" Hands in the air, he kicked away from her as quickly as he could. Wiping the water from his face, he said, "That'll teach me to mess with you."

"You got that right." Despite her tough talk, she struggled to contain her smile.

Meanwhile, her boys were giggling. A sound that was, no doubt, music to her ears after the year they'd had. Especially Grayson.

"That was awesome!" said her eldest.

"Yeah, awesome," echoed Bryce.

Ms. D'Lynn floated through the water, her legs behind her while her arms were draped over the sides of the inner tube. "Who wants to play Marco Polo?"

Four cries of "Me" carried into the still air.

After several rounds, Tessa and her aunt retreated to float beneath the shade of a sprawling live oak limb, while Dirk gave the boys some pointers on snorkeling. Until Grayson announced he was hungry.

"Aunt Dee," he hollered across the way. "Can we have pie now?"

"Grayson, you're always thinking about your stomach." Tessa shook her head.

"Just wait'll he's a teenager." Dirk and his brother had about eaten their parents out of house and home.

Ms. D'Lynn chuckled and started toward the bank. "Come on, Gray, let's go get some celebratory pie."

"Me, too." Bryce kicked his short legs as fast as he could until he caught up with them.

Meanwhile, Tessa joined Dirk on the pier where he was putting on his prosthetic. "Looks like Grayson's not the only one who's hungry."

Grinning, he tossed her a towel. "Swimming makes everyone hungry."

At the table, Ms. D'Lynn served up the chocolate and meringue treat before offering a prayer of thanksgiving for Tessa's new job.

With Nash napping under the table, she eyed Grayson. "Gray, what are you looking forward to most about living at the ranch?"

He thought for a moment. "Helping Mr. Dirk."

The comment had Dirk smiling. "I'm looking forward to that, too. But what about school?"

The kid slouched. "Aw, I forgot about that. Can I still help you sometimes?"

"Of course you can."

"Bryce," their aunt started, "what about you?"

"Playing with Owen. And Mr. Dirk." He nodded.

Dirk's heart swelled. He couldn't recall the last time he'd been this happy. Tessa and her boys had amplified his life. He never dreamed he'd be this content again.

Turning her attention to her niece, Ms. D'Lynn said, "And you, Tessa?"

"I'm just eager to see what the future might hold."

While the statement seemed rather generic, the look she sent Dirk only intensified what he already felt for her. The fact that they were able to connect on so many different levels and could readily share their failures and disappointments as easily as their triumphs and happiness had created a bond that was impossible to ignore.

All too soon, the oppressive late-afternoon heat had the boys and their aunt returning to the water with Nash. Molly, on the other hand, remained in the nearby shade while Tessa and Dirk stayed behind to clean up. Although, he might've had ulterior motives.

Closing the lid on the cooler, Tessa peered up at him. "Thank you for everything you've done these past few days. If it hadn't been for you, I'd still be going in circles, trying to decide what to do first."

He took hold of her hand, entwining their fingers as he tugged her closer. "You're welcome. Though I'll admit, my reasons were purely selfish."

Narrowing her gaze, she shook her head. "How can you say that after all the work you've had to do these past few days?"

"Because I want you to stay." Lifting her hand, he briefly pressed his lips to her knuckles.

She continued to watch him. "Selfish or not, it was you who gave me the courage to pursue my dream of living here at Legacy Ranch. And now it's becoming a reality."

With her boys' laughter echoing from the water, he lowered her hand as they both looked that way.

"I'm confident this is where God wants us. Because for the first time in a very long while, we're all genuinely happy."

Staring into her eyes again, he knew just how she felt.

Molly's sudden barking jolted him, chasing the fanciful thoughts away. That wasn't her usual bark. This was emphatic and persistent.

Dirk looked down the pier as Molly took off.

At the end, Nash moved back and forth at a frenzied pace, barking.

Then Molly jumped into the water.

"Oh, no." Something was wrong. Dreadfully wrong. He whisked past Tessa and propelled himself along the long stretch of wood as fast as he could.

Ms. D'Lynn had abandoned her float and was swimming toward the pier, her strokes fast and furious, obviously seeing something he couldn't.

Behind him, Dirk heard Tessa's footfalls rapidly approaching as he reached the edge of the pier. Looking into the water, his heart all but stopped when he saw Grayson face down. And from the looks of things, he was unconscious.

Ms. D'Lynn was drawing closer while Bryce looked on with wide eyes.

Dropping to his knees, Dirk realized Molly had, somehow, maneuvered herself beneath the boy, and was holding Grayson's head above the water with her own.

"Grayson!" Tessa stopped beside Dirk.

On his belly now, he reached into the water with both hands, grabbing hold of her son's swim-shirt-covered torso.

Tessa hopped into the water as her aunt neared.

When Molly paddled out of the way, Tessa and her aunt rolled Grayson onto his back. Then managed to lift him just enough for Dirk to grab him under the arms. Mustering every ounce of strength he possessed, he pulled the boy onto the pier and laid him down, relieved when he realized the boy was breathing.

"Is he breathing?" A dripping Tessa was beside them now, her own breaths fast and furious.

"Yes."

"Thank God." Pushing the hair away from her son's face, she dropped to her knees. "Grayson. Hey, buddy."

Molly came alongside them, water dripping from her fur.

She whined, nudging the boy with her muzzle, and Grayson groaned.

A moment later, he opened his eyes.

"Grayson?" Encouraged, Tessa lifted his head slightly to cradle it.

"Oooww." The boy winced.

"Sorry." She gently lowered it again, looking up at her aunt and Bryce as they approached. "What happened?"

"He was trying to do a cannonball like Dirk," said Bryce.

"Near as I could tell, he hit his head on the edge of the pier." Ms. D'Lynn rubbed on Molly. "Thank the Lord, this gal was ready to help him."

The woman was right about that. Molly had likely saved Grayson from drowning.

"Mama, you're bleeding." Bryce pointed to Tessa's hand.

Dirk's heart dropped when he realized it wasn't her blood. It was Grayson's.

This was all his fault. If he hadn't been showing off earlier, Grayson wouldn't have attempted this.

*My sister has endured enough pain.* Meredith's words haunted him.

He swallowed the boulder that had lodged in his throat. "We need to get him to the hospital. He might have a concussion."

The words traumatic brain injury had nearly sent Tessa into shock. After all she'd gone through with Nick after his TBI, she never wanted to hear those words again. Thankfully, the doctor on call had given her a thorough explanation and assured her that Grayson's injury was a very mild concussion. Then promptly provided her with a list of things to look out for.

By the grace of God, other than a minor headache the following day, Grayson had been just fine. Which had made it even harder to convince him he still needed to rest.

She'd hoped Dirk might come by to keep Grayson company, or let Molly hang out with him. But she hadn't seen him since he'd dropped her and Grayson off after their trip to the hospital Sunday evening. And while he'd texted Monday, asking how Grayson was doing, she hadn't heard from him since. He hadn't been by the bunkhouse, either. Or responded to any of her texts or voicemails. And it was already Thursday.

She couldn't understand it. Everything had been going so well between her and Dirk. The tender moments they'd shared had brought healing to her wounded heart. They understood each other so well. Why did it feel like he was pulling away?

Those questions and more meant she hadn't accomplished much this week. The shiplap still needed a final coat of paint. She'd removed the boxes from the entry hall but had yet to unpack the majority of them.

Aunt Dee had sat with Grayson Monday so Tessa could drop off her completed paperwork at the HR office in Hope Crossing. A few formalities still needed to take place before Tessa would officially resign from her previous position, though she'd already given her soon-to-be former principal a courtesy call, notifying her of her plans.

Now, with a casserole in the oven—the only thing she'd managed to accomplish today—she joined the boys in the family room where they were watching the first installment of that *Hero Squad* movie Dirk had taken them to see.

"Supper will be ready soon."

Watching her from the sofa, Bryce said, "Is Dirk coming?"

"No, sweetie. I'm afraid not."

"He's probably mad at me for getting hurt." In the recliner, Grayson brooded once again.

Moving alongside him, she said, "Grayson, that is not true. He's just been busy. Remember, he said he had a cabinet installation this week?" Though that had never stopped him before.

"So why hasn't he come after work? Or called?"

He must've read her mind. And she wanted the answers to those questions just as badly as Grayson did.

"I don't know. But I'm sure he has a good explanation." One she was dying to know.

"Something smells delicious. Is that your chicken and rice, Tessa?"

She turned at her aunt's voice to find her standing in the opening between the family room and kitchen, dust covering her usual work clothes. "Yes, ma'am." Standing, she returned to the kitchen and waved her aunt into the dining room.

"Did you hear from Dirk?" The woman looked so hopeful.

"No."

Dee scowled. "Gentry says he thinks he's feelin' guilty." Her aunt looked her in the eye. "That he blames himself for what happened to Grayson."

"I've wondered about that, too. But you'd think he'd call or come by to check on him."

"Hard to tell what's going on in that handsome head of his. Unless..." Dee's eyes met Tessa's. "What if Grayson's accident was like some sort of trigger for Dirk?"

Tessa's gaze narrowed. "How so?"

"Gentry says Dirk blamed himself for what happened to his family. You don't s'pose...?"

The phrase Dirk gave her that day they first started removing the paneling in the living room tumbled through her mind.

*Questioning God's sovereignty can be exhausting. But trusting Him brings hope.*

Tessa pressed her fingertips to her lips. Did what happened to Grayson have Dirk questioning God again?

"Aunt Dee, I hate to ask you this, but would you please watch the boys for me?"

One blond brow arched. "Depends. You goin' to see Dirk?"

"Yes, I am." Though she hated leaving when Grayson was feeling so down, she prayed she might have some good news for him when she returned.

Watching the countryside whiz past on the drive to Dirk's, she thought about all the regret she'd carried over not pushing Nick harder to get help. Or even pulling some sort of intervention. She would not allow regret to consume her again. Not when she and Dirk were on the verge of something that felt so right and promising.

She just hoped he was home. Then again, it wasn't like he had much of a social life. Something she'd once felt bad about. Today, she hoped it played in her favor.

Moving along the dirt road that led to his house, she spotted his truck parked in the drive. She parked and pulled in a deep breath before stepping into the afternoon heat. And as she started toward the door, she realized she hadn't paused long enough to make herself look halfway presentable. Wearing an old T-shirt, paint-spattered shorts, she hadn't even brushed her hair since this morning, let alone given any thought to makeup.

Oh, well. Too late now.

She knocked and waited. When there was no response, she turned into a Peeping Tom once again. Still nothing.

She continued around to his shop. And when she heard noises inside, she knew she'd found him.

Slipping through the door, she saw him leaning over a piece of wood, wearing goggles as he skillfully maneuvered a sander back and forth, Molly at his feet.

When the dog spotted Tessa, she hopped to her feet, tail wagging as she approached.

Then Dirk caught sight of her.

He turned off the sander and removed his goggles. "Tessa? What are you doing here?"

Moving closer to him, she said, "Hoping to find out why you're avoiding me and the boys."

"I'm not avoiding—"

She held up a hand. "Spare me. We've seen you every day for the past I don't know how many weeks, and now you won't even respond to my texts. Why?"

"That cabinet order. I had to install it."

"Had? That sounds like you're done. So when are you coming back to Legacy Ranch to work on the bunkhouse?"

He sucked in a deep breath. "I-I'm not sure." Then she noticed the deep lines carved into his face.

Oh, this was worse than she thought.

"Dirk, please don't do this." She closed the distance between them. "I have two sad little boys who think the world of you. One who believes you're upset with him for getting hurt."

If it was possible, the furrow in his brow deepened. "What? No." He set the sander aside. "How could he believe that?"

"I don't know. I don't understand it, either, any more than I understand why you're blaming yourself." Reaching out, she set her hand on his forearm. "Dirk, Grayson and Bryce love you." She looked into his tormented eyes. "*I* love you, too. And I want to be with you."

He pulled out of her grasp and looked away. "No. I already destroyed my family. I won't destroy yours, too."

Feeling as though she'd been kicked in the stomach, she blinked back tears. "You didn't do anything."

"If I hadn't tried to show off by doing that cannonball, Grayson wouldn't have attempted it, either." He refused to look at her. And it was tearing her apart.

She swallowed the boulder in her throat. "You know, a wise man once gave me some sage advice that helped point me back to God. He said, 'Questioning God's sovereignty can be exhausting. But trusting Him brings hope.'" She sniffed. "You helped restore our hope, Dirk. I'm sorry it cost you yours."

Despite the tears blurring her vision, she turned and started toward the door, not stopping until she was safely inside her vehicle. And as she started the engine, her tears turned to anger. Dirk had given up on her just the way Nick had. Why was it when the going got tough, the men in her life checked out on her? Why wasn't she worth fighting for?

# Chapter Fifteen

Dirk couldn't sleep that night, despite working in his shop well into the wee hours of this morning. How could he with three little words echoing in his mind? *I love you.*

Now as he sat at the island in his kitchen, eyes closed, one palm tightening around his coffee mug while he rubbed Molly with the other, he recognized how much courage it must've taken for Tessa to say those words. And while he'd longed to echo them, he refused to give in to his selfish desires. Tessa and her boys deserved better. They'd suffered enough already.

Picking up his phone, he scrolled for Ms. D'Lynn's name, then hesitated a moment before making the call.

Molly whined beside him.

"I know, girl. I'm going to miss them, too." With one hand on the pup's head, he tapped the call icon on his phone.

"Good mornin', Dirk." Oh, to have Ms. D'Lynn's perpetually positive attitude.

"Morning." He cleared his throat "I-uh… I'm afraid I have some bad news."

Molly stood on her hind legs, setting her front paws atop his thighs.

"Oh?" Ms. D'Lynn's concern came through the line.

He dug his fingers into Molly's fur. "I'm not going to be able to take on the bunkhouse and barn after all."

"I-I'm sorry to hear that. Is there a problem?" Surely she knew.

"I just don't think I could have things done in a timely manner, so it would probably be best if you find another contractor. I'd be happy to send you a couple of names."

"I see." The disappointment in her tone nearly crushed him. "Well, I'm afraid I'm gonna to have to think on that and get back to you."

He rubbed Molly more vigorously. "I understand."

"Dirk?"

He squeezed his eyes shut. "Yes, ma'am."

After a lengthy pause, she said, "If you ever need a reference, I'd be more than happy to give you one."

The scripture verse about turning the other cheek came to mind.

"Thank you, Ms. D'Lynn. I appreciate that."

"You take care, Dirk."

"You, too." He ended the call, feeling like a jerk. But with Tessa and the boys living at the ranch, it would only be a matter of time before he allowed them back into his life. And at what cost to them?

Two loud thuds at the front door let him know his brother was here. Great.

Unable to find the energy to get up, he gave Molly a final pat before catching her eye. "Door."

She dropped to the floor and trotted over, then snagged the rope dangling from the handle between her teeth and pulled the door open.

"Oh, hey, Molly," he heard his brother say. "Thanks." The door closed and Jared's footfalls echoed through the otherwise silent space.

"Dirk…" Jared stopped in front of him, his gaze roaming from Dirk's bedhead to his wrinkled T-shirt and baggy shorts. "What's got you lookin' so rough?"

"Life." He put his cup to his lips and drained the remaining contents.

"Which part of it?" Jared grabbed a mug from the cupboard before reaching for the coffeepot. "Personal or business?"

"In this case, both." Dirk slid his cup across the countertop. "I'll take a refill."

Jared replenished Dirk's before pouring his own, then returned the carafe to the warmer. "If it's both, then it must involve Legacy Ranch and—" he snapped his fingers as he tried to recall "—Tessa! That's her name, right?"

Dirk nodded and took a sip, burning his tongue.

Easing onto the stool beside Dirk's, his brother grew serious. "What happened?"

He told him all that had transpired at the swimming hole.

Jared looked confused. "He's okay, though?"

"Minor concussion." Dirk's hand instinctively went to Molly.

"Oh. Still, kids do reckless things. They get hurt. Look at you and me. How many times did we end up in the ER?"

"Grayson only attempted the cannonball because I'd done one earlier."

Jared popped Dirk in the arm. "Look at you. Showing off for the ladies."

"Yeah and sending her son to the hospital."

Jared cleared his throat. "Sorry."

"If I'd just paid closer attention."

Jared stared into his cup. "Dirk, you said the same thing about the accident."

"Which just goes to prove that I'm a hazard to the people I love and care about."

"Whoa!"

"What?" Dirk looked at his brother, wondering if he'd ever seen Jared so serious.

"You love her." Jared's gaze narrowed. "And what happened to her son reminded you of the accident, didn't it?"

Rubbing Molly a little more aggressively, Dirk stared into his cup. He saw the pouring rain. The semi.

He closed his eyes. Until he felt Jared's hand on his shoulder.

"You're afraid of loving and losing again, aren't you?"

"I should come with a warning label."

"Dirk, God's word says you're fearfully and wonderfully made, not dangerously and dreadfully. It also talks about turning our mourning into dancing. Don't you think you've mourned long enough?"

*It's time for you to accept the past and embrace the future God has for you.* Lindsey's mother's words again played in his mind.

*God, what are You trying to tell me?*

"I don't know, Jared. I think I will always mourn my wife and daughter."

"Fair enough. But do you think Lindsey would want you living your life like a hermit, afraid to open your heart again because of a bunch of what-ifs?" Jared drained his mug and set it on the counter. "Think about it."

With that, he strolled to the door and let himself out.

Dirk stared up at the rafters. *God, I want to believe what everyone is saying, but I'm afraid.*

*Trust.*

Wasn't that what he'd been doing? At least, until Grayson got hurt.

*Questioning God's sovereignty can be exhausting. But trusting Him brings hope.*

He had to hand it to Tessa. Not only had she taken his words to heart, she'd called him out with them. Though his heart hurt when he thought about the pained expression on her face last night.

Shaking it off, he said, "Come on, Molly. I need a shower."

Too bad for him, there was no shaking off Tessa. She was smart and beautiful, a good mother who didn't have time to wallow in her own pain because she was so focused on her boys.

When he returned smelling much better, he headed for the coffeepot and another cup. Until a knock at the door had him shifting directions.

He glanced at Molly. "You don't suppose it's Jared again, do you?"

She barked and trotted toward the door.

"Okay, okay." She was excited about something.

When Dirk opened it, Grayson stood there, his aunt several feet behind him.

Dragging his fingertips across Molly's head, Dirk said, "Grayson, what are you doing here?"

"I had to talk to you." The kid looked frightened.

"Sure. Come on in." His glance moved to Grayson's aunt. "Ms. D'Lynn." He waved her inside. "How are you feeling, Grayson?"

"Good. Sorta."

Closing the door, Dirk looked to Ms. D'Lynn for clarification, but she remained silent.

Grayson was on his knees now, his arms around Molly's neck as he rubbed his cheek against her soft fur.

"I think she's missed you." Dirk smiled.

"I missed her, too," said Grayson.

Meanwhile, Ms. D'Lynn was holding her cowboy hat in place as she tipped her head back to take in the rafters. "So this is what y'all've been talkin' about."

Only then did he realize she'd never been here. "Yes, ma'am."

Lowering her gaze to his, she said, "You are one talented fella, Dirk."

The comment had him smiling. "Thank you." He turned his attention back to Grayson and Molly. "What was it you wanted to talk to me about?"

The boy glanced toward his aunt. Then, with tears in his eyes and both arms still around Molly, he looked up at Dirk. "I heard Aunt Dee telling my mom you weren't coming back to the ranch." His bottom lip quivered. "I wanted to tell you I'm sorry I got hurt. And that I had to go to the hospital. I wasn't trying to cause trouble. I promise."

Dirk knelt beside the boy. "Grayson, you didn't do anything wrong. I was the one who messed up. I set a bad example for you when I tried to show off by doing that cannonball. But none of that has anything to do with me not coming back to the ranch."

Tears spilling onto his cheeks, he looked at Dirk. "Then why? Don't you like us anymore?"

"Of course I like you. It's just…complicated."

"That's what my mom said." He stood then, keeping one hand on Molly. "But I don't want you to leave. Our family is better with you." He was crying in earnest now. "You made my mom smile again. And my grandparents." He threw his arms around Dirk's neck and held on tight. "I love you, Dirk."

Once he got over the shock, Dirk said, "I love you, too, Grayson." And with his arms around the boy, Dirk felt something shift inside of him. Like something that was stuck had finally loosened, filling him with more love than he'd ever imagined he could feel again. "Don't you worry," he whispered into the boy's hair. "I'm going to fix this. You just need to be patient, okay?"

He felt Grayson's nod.

With a final hug, Dirk stood and looked at Ms. D'Lynn. The tough cowgirl had tears rolling down her cheeks. But he wasn't about to point that out for fear she might hurt him.

Swiping them away, she said, "We serve a God of second chances, Dirk. And while you may feel unworthy, I believe He's given you and Tessa a gift." She sniffed and straightened. "Come on, Grayson. We need to get you back home."

Dirk opened the door as Grayson gave Molly one last hug.

Meanwhile, Ms. D'Lynn paused beside him. Leaning closer, she whispered, "Just remember, the thing about a gift is that you have to be willing to accept it. Otherwise, both the giver and the receiver get cheated out of a blessing."

Perched on the edge of the bed in her room, Tessa hit the send button, submitting her official letter of resignation to her old school. Not that she hadn't contemplated going back to Houston. Then she realized that was a coward's way of thinking. She'd be cheating her sons of the opportunity to live out their dreams. Not to mention sacrificing her own.

She'd dreamed of living at Legacy Ranch long before she ever met Dirk. Though he was the one who'd given her the courage to follow that dream. Perhaps that was why God had brought Dirk into her life. To encourage her to step out in faith. Though, he'd done so much more. He'd helped her family heal and provided a safe haven for Grayson. Because of Dirk's willingness to listen, she had her son back. And for that, she would be eternally grateful.

She smiled, staring out the window at the cattle-dotted land. *Thank You, God, for bringing Dirk into our lives. He routinely pointed me back to You. And because of him, my family is whole again.*

She drew in a shuddering breath. *He also showed me that I could love again. Even if he's not the man for me, I know that I'm capable of opening my heart to whatever possibilities You might put in my path.* She worried her bottom lip. *Still, getting over him is going to be tough. So, please, help me and my boys to heal. Help me be the mom my boys need. Thank You, Jesus. Amen.*

Standing, she smiled and placed her laptop on the nightstand, feeling lighter. Hopeful, even. Then she hurried downstairs, where her aunt and the boys were enjoying ice cream at the kitchen table.

Tessa eyed the old schoolhouse clock. "Guess this means we're either having a late or light supper."

"We're celebrating." Grayson smiled behind a chocolate mustache.

"Celebrating what?"

With Nash stretched out on the floor, watching her hopefully, Aunt Dee wiped her mouth with a napkin. "That your job is now official."

"So you're celebrating without me?"

Dee motioned toward the refrigerator. "Feel free to fix yourself a bowl and join us."

While she found their logic a bit backward… "You know what, I think I just might do that."

She moved to the freezer and was about to pull out the container of cookies and cream when there was a knock at the front door.

Nash woofed and hopped to his feet.

Setting a hand atop the dog, Dee said, "Tessa, would you mind gettin' that, please?"

"O-kay." She hastily returned the ice cream to the freezer

before making her way into the center hall. And when she opened the door, her breath caught.

Dirk stood there, wearing tan shorts and a navy blue T-shirt that highlighted those gorgeous eyes of his, and he was holding a bouquet of red roses. At his side, Molly looked as though she was smiling.

Suddenly conscious of her own attire—paint-spattered shorts and a baggy T-shirt—Tessa found herself holding on to the door for fear she might fall over. "Dirk. What are you doing here?"

"I wanted to give you these." He held out the flowers. "And I was wondering if you'd take a little walk with me."

She brought the bouquet to her nose, savoring their delightful fragrance while willing herself not to read too much—if anything—into the gesture. "You know it's, like, ninety-eight degrees, right?"

He looked away then, shifting his weight to his good leg. "Do…you suppose we could go to the cabin?"

Despite her determination not to get her hopes up, her nerve endings tingled. "Let me see if Aunt Dee will watch the boys."

"Yep," her aunt responded from the kitchen. "We're good here. Y'all go on."

Had she been eavesdropping?

"Feel free to leave Molly," Dee continued. "Wouldn't want her to get heat stroke."

Why did Tessa get the feeling her aunt was up to something? Or, perhaps, just trying to play matchmaker.

Grayson appeared at the other end of the hall. "Come on, Molly." He patted his thighs.

The dog looked up at Dirk as if asking permission.

"Go ahead, girl."

Tessa set the roses aside before closing the door and following Dirk to his truck.

As he turned on the engine and the air conditioning sprang to life, he said, "Are things settled with your new job yet?"

"Yes. As a matter of fact, I just sent off my letter of resignation."

His smile grew wide. "Congratulations."

"Thank you." She picked at a bit of dried paint on her shirt, wishing she was wearing something a little more attractive than work clothes. Sure, the shiplap in the dining room was finally complete, but she was sweaty and gross while Dirk looked like a handsomely rugged cover model.

They pulled up to the cabin, parking in the shade of the old live oak. After making their way onto the porch, she punched the code into the new keypad lock she'd suggested her aunt have installed so they wouldn't have to worry about guest keys.

Dirk gestured for her to go first, then followed her into the blessedly cooler air.

"Wow…" His gaze traversed the space that now boasted a leather-look sofa and a cozy upholstered chair, along with an area rug and accent pieces. "This place looks great."

"Doesn't it, though?" She couldn't help smiling. "My aunt's dream has finally come to life." Her gaze settled on Dirk. "And we appreciate all of your help."

"It was my pleasure." Peering up to the loft with its antique-looking metal bed, he added, "I love to see transformations like this. Taking something most people would think unsalvageable and then uncovering its natural charm."

"You did a wonderful job." Rubbing her arms, she moved past the sofa to stand behind it, eager to know why he was here. "So, what's on your mind?"

"You."

Her gaze darted to his as he moved beside her, erasing that distance she'd hoped to maintain.

He reached into his pocket. "I want you to have this."

She felt her eyes widen when he held up a white gold band set with diamonds.

"It's a promise that I will always be forthcoming with you," he continued. "About my fears and doubts, as well as my dreams and desires. Because you are my dream and my desire, Tessa. And though I may not feel worthy of your love, that's not for me to decide. I love you, Tessa. I want to share my life with you. To help you raise Grayson and Bryce. To be there for all of you, good or bad, no matter what life throws our way. Will you allow me to be that man?"

Swallowing around the lump lodged in her throat, she said, "Perhaps." She squared her shoulders. "But I have some conditions."

"Okay." His eyes were still riveted to hers.

"That you will let me be there for you, as well. Good or bad. Because like it says in Ecclesiastes, 'Two are better than one. For if they fall, the one will lift up his fellow. But woe to him that is alone when he falleth; for he hath not another to pick him up.'" She moved closer. "We both fell when we were alone. But these last couple of months we've picked each other up."

"And we were stronger for it." His Adam's apple bobbed. "Until I chose to stand alone." He palmed her cheek, and she leaned into it. "I'm sorry I turned you away, Tessa." His gray-blue eyes bore into hers. "Please say you'll forgive me."

"Of course I will."

He kissed her then, and as she wound her arms around his neck she kissed him right back with a fervor she hoped would erase any doubts of her feelings for him.

When they parted, he took hold of her left hand and slid

the band on her ring finger. "I'm not going to rush you into anything. I know your life is kind of hectic right now." Still holding her hands, he looked into her eyes. "But from this day forward, I am yours. And I will always be there for you and your sons. I love you."

Pushing up on her toes, she kissed him. "I love you, too. However, I think we should get back to the house, because I know there's at least one person, if not three, who's dying to know what's happening between us right now."

With his arms around her waist, he tugged her closer. "Let's make them wait a little while longer."

# *Epilogue*

Tessa's days of battling traffic going to and from school were over. Just one of many things she appreciated about living at Legacy Ranch.

She'd never seen her boys so happy. Six weeks into the school year, and both had already made a host of new friends. Meanwhile, the staff had made Tessa feel right at home, making their move almost flawless.

After Dirk's promise/proposal and sharing the news with the boys and Aunt Dee, as well as the rest of their families—including Dan and Gina, who seemed delighted—Tessa went ahead and put her house in Houston on the market, where it sold within days. Of course, that meant they had to get everything out of it. Thankfully, Dirk's parents had an old storage container at their place and offered to let her store things there.

While Dirk continued his work on the bunkhouse and discussions for the barn dragged on, the two of them had also been scouring every part of Legacy Ranch, looking for the perfect spot to build their home. Someplace on a bluff overlooking the ranch, with majestic oak trees and a view that went on forever. And while they'd found a couple of spots that were okay, they were still holding out for the one that felt just right.

One thing they had decided on, though, was a wedding date. And since both of their families would be coming together for the first time this third Saturday in September, she and Dirk would finally share it with them.

With a late-summer heat ridge perched over the area, the swimming hole seemed the perfect place to gather for lunch and some fun. Meredith, Audrey and Kendall had arrived yesterday to help with preparations. Meanwhile, Dirk's parents, John and Linda, had just arrived, along with Jared, Hannah and their two children, Ava and Zac.

"What a beautiful spot." Linda took in the freshly mowed area with two tablecloth-covered picnic tables, another table laden with ice chests full of food and a cornhole setup, in addition to the sparkling waters of the swimming hole itself.

"I'll say." Her husband pointed to the water. "Spring fed?"

"You betcha," Aunt Dee said with a wink. "That cool water is great for the circulation."

"I doubt that'll stop the kids." Hannah eyed her eight-year-old son and six-year-old daughter at the water's edge with Grayson, Bryce and Molly.

"With this heat, I doubt it'll stop any of us," added Jared.

The introductions continued with Tessa's sisters before Dirk said, "Who's ready to hit the water?"

Soon, everyone was either floating or splashing about. Most of the women opted to float. Tessa welcomed the opportunity to slip off to one side and chat with Dirk's mother and sister-in-law.

"Tessa," Linda began, "I want to thank you for bringing my son back to life. Until you and your boys came along, I felt like Dirk was just existing. Now, he's truly living again."

"Aww, Linda. I kind of feel the same way about Dirk." Her gaze instinctively sought him out as he played Marco Polo with the kids. "My boys and I were struggling to stay afloat before he came into our lives. He gets me. And isn't afraid to challenge me, particularly in my faith."

"Well, I am just thrilled that you, Grayson and Bryce will be joining our family."

"Have you two set a wedding date yet?" Hannah watched her expectantly.

Tessa carefully selected her words, not wanting to divulge too much just yet. "I believe an agreement has been reached and details will be forthcoming in the very near future."

The women chuckled.

"If I didn't know better," said Hannah, "I'd think you were a lawyer instead of a teacher."

When Aunt Dee hollered, "Come and get it," a short time later, nobody wasted any time.

Seemingly having worked up an appetite, everyone gathered around the picnic tables in short order. And after a brief prayer, they all dug in to a variety of sandwiches, salads, fruit and fresh-squeezed lemonade.

Then, while most everyone satiated their sweet tooth with Aunt Dee's peach cobbler, Dirk took hold of Tessa's hand, urging her to stand with him. And she liked it when he didn't let go.

"So, we have an announcement." With Molly at his side, his gaze met hers, sending her heart into overdrive.

Shifting his attention to their families, he continued. "We've set a wedding date."

He seemed to defer to her then, nudging her with his elbow.

"Oh!" She smiled. "We will be wed on March the eighth." Just as her and the boys' spring break would be getting started. With this being her first year at the school, she didn't want to take time off for her wedding. "It'll be a small affair, since this is a second wedding for both of us."

"Where?" Aunt Dee asked.

Glancing at her grinning betrothed, Tessa said, "Where do you think?"

"Hot dog!" Dee smacked her hands together. "We're gonna host our first weddin' at the ranch."

"Dirk," Audrey hollered, "think we can have the barn done by then?"

Shaking his head, he said, "I think that's pushing things." Especially when Aunt Dee was still deciding. Though she was leaning toward the idea of a venue.

After spending a little more time in and out of the water, Dirk's family departed, but not before Linda and Aunt Dee had exchanged phone numbers.

Back at the house, Tessa helped her aunt and sisters unpack things while Dirk parked in front of *Hero Squad* with the boys, Molly and Nash.

Then just about the time she was ready to sit down and put her feet up, Dirk came alongside her.

"Care to go for a little ride?"

She was tempted to say no, until he added, "Just the two of us."

"Sure, let's go."

After letting Aunt Dee know they were leaving and getting permission to take the utility vehicle, Tessa let Dirk drive while Molly sat between them.

"I have something I want to show you," he said over the engine noise.

She simply nodded and smiled, weary, yet content.

"I think I might have found our perfect home site."

Straightening, she twisted her head his way. "Really? Where?"

He chuckled. "I'm about to show you."

As they bounded across the open pasture toward the back of the property, she felt all tingly inside. "I can't wait."

"Now, you're going to have to use your imagination."

Wait, he was showing her an imaginary house site? "Dirk, did you really find something, or is this just an excuse to get me alone?"

Grinning, he said, "Would you be mad at me if I said both?"

She arched a brow, knowing she could never be mad at him.

Dirk eased to the top of a gentle rise then stopped in front of something that looked like it might be a tree, but spindly yaupon holly stood like a wall in front of it. And at the top was a giant dome of green.

Coming to a stop, he turned off the engine. "Come with me."

Shielding her eyes from the sun, she slid out of the vehicle, Molly bounding beside her.

Several feet away, Dirk gestured to the so-called tree. "This is where you're going to have to use your imagination."

Glancing up at him as though he'd lost his marbles, she said, "What do you mean?"

"Okay, just take this in for a second. Top to bottom. All around."

She reluctantly complied. "Alright."

Taking hold of her hand, he smiled. "Now come with me."

They walked until the yaupon made it impossible to go any farther.

Then Dirk stretched out his arms to spread the skinny trees as far apart as possible. "Look in there and tell me what you see."

She glanced about until she recognized a very large tree

trunk. It looked like it had thick arms stretching every which way. "Is that a live oak?"

"It sure is."

Stepping back, she lifted her gaze to the green dome. "But where's its top? Its leaves?"

"Hidden behind all of those grapevines."

"No way."

"Yes way. And look at this."

When he turned her around, she looked down to see cattle and pastureland that went on forever. "Legacy Ranch."

"In all her glory." He slipped an arm around her waist. "What do you think?"

Smiling so big her cheeks hurt, she said, "I think we just found the place for our home."

He turned her to face him, cupping her cheek in his palm. "In that case, welcome home, Tessa."

\* \* \* \* \*

Dear Reader,

The loss of a loved one is always difficult. But when tragedy is involved, that grief is often accompanied by guilt and
second-guessing. And so it was with Dirk and Tessa. But
God, even in our heartache and questioning, He is there,
if we will just call on Him. His word tells us His compas-
sions never fail.

I hope you enjoyed this first journey to Legacy Ranch.
My husband's great-grandmother was the inspiration for this
series. She and her sister were orphaned in 1873 when a yellow fever epidemic took their parents, and they went to live
with their uncle. A few years later, her sister died.

Prior to his death, their father had purchased a large plot of
land for his daughters. Back in those days, her uncle could've
easily sold it, but he held on to it for my husband's great-
grandmother. And because of his compassion for his orphaned niece, my husband and I are blessed to call a portion
of that original land home.

I hope you'll join me as the stories of Tessa's sisters are
revealed in the coming months. Until then, I'd love to connect with you. You can email me at Mindy@MindyOben-
haus.com, or join me on Facebook at authormindyobenhaus
or Instagram @mindy.obenhaus.

Until next time,
*Mindy*